José Margati

A Trip to the City of Mexico.

José Margati

A Trip to the City of Mexico.

ISBN/EAN: 9783742811387

Manufactured in Europe, USA, Canada, Australia, Japa

Cover: Foto ©Andreas Hilbeck / pixelio.de

Manufactured and distributed by brebook publishing software
(www.brebook.com)

José Margati

A Trip to the City of Mexico.

A TRIP

TO THE

CITY OF MEXICO.

BY

JOSÉ MARGATI.

—

"Jam tempus agit res."

PUBLISHED BY

PUTNAM, MESSERVY & CO.
Bankers,
60 STATE STREET, BOSTON.

1885.

FRANK WOOD, PRINTER, BOSTON.

It has often been suggested to me to give in print some account of the Mexican Central Excursion. Feeling that this was a grand opportunity for a skilful pen upon an interesting subject, and that the requisite talent for the purpose was not lacking in our party, I was reluctant to undertake the work, until sufficient time had elapsed to satisfy me, at least, that unless I took it upon myself it might remain unwritten, and for-ever lost, except to the memory of a few of those who, like myself, participated in it.

This story, which must of necessity be in the form of a diary of events, is made up largely from private memoranda which were made day after day, with the sole object of refreshing the memory, when relating an account of the journey upon my return home. In rewriting my diary, however, I have made use of all the material I could gather, and from whatever source, which could be woven into my story, to make it as complete a record of that delightful excursion as possible. Some of the speeches herein quoted were translated from Mexican papers, and I believe them to be authentic reports of what was really said at the time. For much of the interesting matter and valuable information which is here given, I am indebted to individual members of the party.

If I have succeeded in weaving together the daily events of that journey in such a manner as to make it interesting, as well as authentic, and at the same time have afforded my travelling companions any pleasure, I shall feel fully repaid for the labor of preparing this little memento.

A COMPLETE LIST OF THE PARTY.

D. ALDEN	*Augusta, Me.*
CHAS. C. BLODGETT	*Boston, Mass.*
E. W. CONVERSE	" "
THOMAS DANA	" "
JACOB EDWARDS	" "
W. P. ELLISON	" "
THOS. G. FROTHINGHAM	" "
FREDERIC R. GUERNSEY	" "
A. B. LAWRIE	" "
FRANK MORISON	" "
A. S. MARCH	" "
THOS. NICKERSON	" "
Mrs. THOS. NICKERSON	" "
R. M. PULSIFER	" "
L. G. PRATT	" "
CHAS. W. PIERCE	" "
A. A. POPE	" "
ALEX. H. RICE	" "
WM. ROTCH	" "
ARTHUR ROTCH	" "
ALDEN SPEARE	" "
ARTHUR SEWALL	" "
S. S. SLEEPER	" "
GEO. B. WILBUR	" "
A. D. WELD	" "
JOSÉ MARGATI	*Salem, Mass.*
FRANK JONES	*Portsmouth, N. H.*
LEVI Z. LEITER	*Chicago, Ill.*
CLARENCE P. DRESSER	" "
CHAS. S. SMITH	*New York, N. Y.*

ALL RAIL EXCURSION TO MEXICO.

MEXICO is now brought under the influence of the progressive nineteenth-century spirit of her sister republic, through the construction of railways connecting the principal cities of the two countries. Places that a few years ago were practically as remote as the two hemispheres, are now only a few hours apart by rail transportation.

A party consisting of about twenty-five well-known gentlemen, capitalists, — some of whom are directors of the newly completed Mexican Central Railroad, and most of them largely interested in it, — left Boston on the evening of the 28th of April, 1884, for an excursion to the City of Mexico, where a banquet, in honor of the completion of the railroad, had been tendered to the party by members of the city government.

The tourists occupied two new Pullman sleeping-cars — the Aguas Calientes and the Aragon — said to have been built specially for the use of the Mexican Central Railroad. They were alike in every respect, very handsome, and well provided with everything necessary to insure the comfort of their occupants during a long journey.

The journey was made without the slightest inconvenience to any of the party, and without the occurrence of a single disagreeable incident — thanks to the very efficient management of a member of the board of directors of the Mexican Central Railroad who piloted the party through.

The route chosen for the excursion was *via* Fitchburg Railroad through the tunnel; New York, West Shore, and Buffalo; Great Western Division Grand Trunk; Chicago, Burlington, and Quincy; Hannibal and St. Jo.; Atchison, Topeka, and Santa Fé; and Mexican Central Railroad.

Notwithstanding the oft-circulated reports of annoyances of a belligerent nature, to which all travellers to Mexico may be subjected, few, if any, of the excursionists had provided themselves with arms for defence; and throughout the journey no arms were necessary for that purpose. Whether the party had received timely warning from reading the Denver *Republican*, or no, they, one and all, had provided themselves instead with a determination not to grumble under any circumstances; for it is a well-known fact that one grumbler or fault-finder can, and often does, destroy the pleasure of a whole party, while one jolly, good-natured, and always pleasant man binds all the party to him with bonds of friendship that are not soon broken or forgotten.

There was no dining-car attached to the train, excepting at rare intervals along the route; but the Buffet cars, which we occupied, were both well provided with everything needful to furnish their occupants with a light repast whenever, on the journey, it was not possible to find a convenient station to stop at for a good square meal.

On Tuesday, the 29th of April, the party took breakfast at the station in Syracuse, N. Y.; after which they were entertained by the Hon. ex-Governor of Massachusetts, a very estimable member of the party, with a vivid and interesting account of the battle of " Bullrun," which he had the rare opportunity to witness, and with other entertaining anecdotes. The view from the car windows offered nothing of any particular interest here, after viewing the extensive salt-works at Syracuse, excepting the four distinct tracks of the New York Central Railroad, which run about parallel with theNew York, West Shore, and Buffalo, its competitor, and which was visible for a long distance of the way.

Suspension bridge was reached at about 4 P. M. At this point a dining-car was attached to the train, which furnished a substantial dinner to all who desired it, avoiding the necessity of stopping extra time at the station for this purpose, which they were anxious not to do, in view of the fact that the train was already some hours behind time.

At 11.15 P. M. the larger part of the party had quietly retired to their respective compartments to rest, when the train stopped, and without any jarring or the least commotion, the cars were put aboard of the ferry, and taken across to Port Huron. A practical illustration of the swiftness of time when in pleasing company, was this night experienced by three of the gentlemen of this party when they suddenly became aware

that it was already past midnight, so well had they
been entertained with a graphic description of Egypt,
and its wonderful pyramids, by one of their number, a
prominent dry-goods merchant from New York.

Wednesday, April 30th. The excursionists were
called at 7.15 A. M., shortly after passing Lansing, the
capital of Michigan, that they might have time to prepare for breakfast, which awaited the arrival of the
train at Battle Creek. This place was reached at
8 o'clock, at least six hours late. After breakfast,
for which ample time was allowed, the train proceeded
on its course to Chicago, where we arrived at about
2.30 P. M. We were so much behind time that we
could only remain one hour at this place instead of
four hours, as originally planned.

Two gentlemen, Mr. Charles W. Pierce, of Boston,
who is largely interested in railroads, and Mr. Levi Z.
Leiter, a former member of the house of Field, Leiter
& Co., of Chicago, a director in the Mexican Central
Railroad, and a very successful merchant, joined the
party at this point. It was designed that our two cars
should connect here with the regular train leaving Chicago daily at 12.15 P. M. for Kansas City; but as we
arrived too late to do this, an arrangement was made
for a special train, consisting of the dining-car Denver,
and a baggage-car, in addition to the Aragon and
Aguas Calientes; and at 3.50 P. M., well provided
with motive power, we left Chicago for Kansas City at
a rapid rate, making only such stops as were necessary
to allow our powerful iron steed time to drink. It was

frequently reported during that evening, that we were going at the rate of sixty miles an hour ; and as several of the gentlemen were experienced railroad-men, there is no occasion to doubt their report. The fact is, to the inexperienced this might seem a moderate estimate of the speed, judging by the rapidity with which we passed objects in the immediate vicinity.

After leaving Chicago an excellent dinner, consisting of soup, boiled salmon, roasts, vegetables, salad, game, fruit, pastry, ices, and delicious coffee was furnished in the dining-car Denver. This was indeed a delightful way to travel, and one calculated to spoil us for any ordinary mode of travelling ever after : indeed, it seemed almost incredible ; here we were being sumptuously fed, in luxurious apartments, and all the while moving rapidly, without the least inconvenience or anxiety to ourselves.

Thursday, May 1st. We passed during the night the regular train, which left Chicago nearly four hours in advance of ours, and have arrived ahead of that train a half-hour or more. The dining-car Denver again was called into requisition this morning, and it furnished an excellent breakfast. We reached Kansas City at 8.30 A. M., and, although it was raining quite hard at the time, several of the gentlemen improved the opportunity by taking carriages and riding about the principal parts of the city for an hour.

Kansas City, though in Missouri, is the trade-centre of the great State whose name it bears. It is the principal eastern terminus of the Atchison, Topeka, and

Santa Fé Railroad, the largest city between St. Louis and San Francisco, and the greatest railroad centre in the West; population nearly one hundred thousand. It is situated on a bend of the Missouri River, where the stream swings round from a southerly course toward the Mississippi, and is the nearest point on the river to the great Southwest, of which it is the principal commercial metropolis. This led to its becoming, half a century ago, the most prominent post in the Santa Fé overland trade. Outfitting for the Mexican War, in 1846, was largely done in Kansas City, and this point was also the principal outfitting station for the California migration in 1849. In 1872, the national depression then prevailing was felt, and there was little growth till 1876, when business began to revive; and since then there has been a most wonderful development, the population increasing from 35,000 to what it is at the present time — 100,000.

Kansas City is the largest depot for agricultural implements in the world. Here, also, manufactures flourish, and consist of such branches as smelting works, rolling-mills, foundries, piano manufactories, glucose works, chemical works, stove works, carriage works, shoe manufactories, breweries, flouring mills, paint manufactories, marble and granite works, brick manufactories, type foundries, and scores of other manufacturing industries, giving employment to thousands of men and millions of capital. It has a board of trade, which, as an organization, has contributed largely to the prosperity of the city. Business is mainly in the hands of young men, whose enterprise and ambition have made Kansas City one of the most prosperous and flourishing cities on the continent; schools are excellent; the daily press compares favorably with that of any other city of the same size in the Union; nearly all religious denominations are here represented, and the general health of the population is above the average.

The railway station seems to be a centre, whence trains for San Francisco, Mexico, New Orleans, and other distant points radiate daily. It had the appearance of being a very busy place, but there was no confusion, and no one seemed to be in any great hurry, and trains moved in and out upon a perfect labyrinth of rails without the least disturbance. Mr. A. A. Robinson, the able manager of the Atchison, Topeka, and Santa Fé Railroad, was at the station, attending personally to the wants of our party.

Mr. Alden Speare, of Boston, a gentleman who has for a long time been connected with the Atchison road as one of its managing directors, joined the party at Kansas City. He occupied a room in Car 99 of the Atchison Railroad, which was here attached to the rear of the train. This was a managing director's car, and it was an elegant affair. The two ends were designed for observation, with long windows of large-sized plate-glass reaching nearly to the floor, and furnished with a dining-table in the centre, a lounge, chairs, a desk, and closets. The middle portion of the car was divided into three bedrooms, excepting a narrow passage on one side. Each room was furnished with double bed, washstand, water-closet, and every convenience that might be looked for in any well-conducted hotel, and the entire car was finished in walnut. An excellent opportunity was here given for observation from the rear of this car — a privilege which was freely offered, and gratefully indulged in by all the members of the party ; and the view from those rear windows as the train sped along was indeed magnificent.

And now, with the train increased by this Car 99,— the comforts of which were shared by others of the party, with its principal occupant previously referred to,— and with the addition, also, of one other gentlemen, Mr. Clarence P. Dresser, of Chicago, who is connected with the Chicago *Eye* as a special correspondent, we left Kansas City at about 10.20 A. M., to continue our route.

Soon after leaving, and becoming fairly settled in one's section for a journey, the enormous distance covered by the Atchison, Topeka, and Santa Fé becomes a matter for reflection. It has an interesting history. It was definitely projected and persistently built through a howling wilderness — a result few men of that day would have been bold enough to prophesy. It now extends from Kansas City to the port of Guaymas, on the western coast of Mexico, and to El Paso, where its track is continuous with that of the Mexican Central, which is, in effect, the extension of its line unbroken to the City of Mexico. Its line extends across the farms and orchards of Eastern Kansas, traverses the Arkansas Valley for nearly four hundred miles, crosses the southeastern corner of Colorado, passes over the entire length of New Mexico from north to

south, and finally places its passengers beyond the
southern boundary of the United States, and upon foreign soil. A gentleman of our party who has long
been connected with this vast enterprise remembers
when, fifteen years ago, all this Western country,
which now is so productive, was useless and unavail-
able. Through its whole extent there was not a
soul to be found, and there was not while the line was
being built. Lands which were as productive then as
they are to-day could not be sold, for the simple reason
that purchasers had no way of marketing their products except by the slow and expensive ox-team.
And now look at the enormous change that has taken
place in so short a time through the agency of this
road! Look at the large increase of population, and
the immensity of the crops that are produced annually,
and will any one question the propriety of the land
grant? In 1870 Kansas did not raise enough wheat to
feed its own population of 365,000, and the bulk of its
territory was not worth pre-emption at $1.25 an acre.
To-day 1,000,000 people in Kansas hold their agricultural lands at twenty-five times their value in 1870
(land that was not worth pre-emption now being
wanted at $30 and $40 an acre), and raise one eleventh
of the wheat crop of the United States and one eighth
of the corn crop. The United States Agricultural
Bureau estimates the Kansas wheat crop this year at
from 48,000,000 to 50,000,000 bushels, and the corn
crop at the enormous figures of 250,000,000 bushels.

We are now moving again rapidly toward Topeka,
our next stopping-place, and where we are expected to

dine. In the meantime let us enter the train, in imag-
ination, that we may see who the gentlemen are that
compose the party, and that are to be our companions
for the next three weeks; and that we may also form
some idea of the manner in which they pass away the
time on a long trip like this, particularly as there are
no ladies present to enliven conversation with their
pure and characteristic humor, or to draw the tribute
of pleasantry which is due them from the sterner sex.
We will begin by entering the first Buffet car, the
Aragon, and going through a narrow passage, richly
ornamented with mirrors, we find a small drawing-room
at our right, which is occupied by two young men; one
of whom, a special correspondent of the Boston *Herald*, is engaged in preparing a dispatch to be forwarded
to Boston by wire from Topeka, or the next telegraph
station we may chance to stop at. This dispatch will
appear in the evening edition of that enterprising news-
paper this very day. It is to him that our families
and friends are indebted for information concerning
the progress of this excursion, which is given twice
each day through the columns of the *Herald*. The
other of these occupants appears to be surrounded
with maps and consular reports, evidently obtaining
information of some sort with relation to Mexico. He
is a Spanish gentleman, long since naturalized in the
United States; he hopes to assist in ascertaining the
opportunities offered for the introduction of American
textile fabrics into Mexico. We will not disturb these
gentlemen by entering the room, but turning aside, we
find ourselves at the foot of a passageway through the

centre of the car. Immediately upon our right sits a
gentleman whose animated glance attracts our attention. He is the president of the largest bicycle firm in
the world, a man of wealth, and largely interested in
the Mexican and other roads. During the war he
served with much gallantry, and was colonel of a
Massachusetts regiment. The ex-Mayor of Newton
sits at our left, engaged in friendly conversation with
his townsman, the well-known agent in Boston for the
sale of a celebrated foreign thread. Further, toward
the centre of the car, we notice four gentlemen intent
upon a game of whist, which is well under way. One of
those facing us is a wealthy Boston gentleman, long
experienced in the dry-goods trade, treasurer of various
manufacturing corporations in the State of Maine, and
a director in the Mexican Central road; he is playing
with the gentleman from New York, the representative
of the Arkwright Club, for his partner. Their oppo-
nents are the Hon. ex-Member of Congress from New
Hampshire, who has large real estate and railroad interests — a wealthy brewer; and his partner is one of
the largest capitalists in Boston, a gentleman who has
long been engaged in the wholesale grocery business,
and is interested in many of the best railroads in the
country. At the remote end of this parlor we find the
wealthy Boston merchant who was one of the pioneers
of trade beyond the Mississippi, than whom, probably,
no member of the party has had a more adventurous
career, having made many journeys among the Indian-
traders of the far West during his early life. There
are also two others, one of whom is a capitalist of

Newton, Mass., formerly in the grocery business, and now largely interested in the Mexican Central, the Atchison, and other railroads; the other, the younger of them, whose clear, ringing voice may be heard all over the car, is one of the wealthiest and most successful merchants of Chicago, and a director in the Mexican Central.

We now proceed out of this car through a narrow passage similar to the one by which we entered, except that we pass at our left the little room where Tom prepares a variety of things well calculated to refresh the inner man, and also the smoking-room. Stopping here, for a moment only, to greet two young men from Chicago, the representatives of leading newspapers in the United States, we cross over the platform into the car Aguas Calientes.

This, as already stated elsewhere, is similar to the Aragon in design and finish. We find the drawing-room occupied by a gentleman, a civil engineer by profession, and a man of large wealth. He is also a director in the Mexican Central road, and it is to him that we are indebted for all the care and management of this excursion. Seated with him is his cousin, a Boston architect, who has built some of the costliest houses at the "Hub." It is to be hoped that the public will some day be permitted to see his valuable collection of sketches along the route. Entering the parlor, we must not omit to pay our respects to the Hon. ex-Governor of Massachusetts, whom we discover seated and reading immediately upon our right. The one sitting opposite to the Governor is a gentleman

practising as an attorney in Boston, who was for two
years a director in the Mexican Central road, and is
still largely interested in it. Here, also, is a whist party
engaged in by well-known gentlemen. One of those facing us is the publisher of the Boston *Daily Herald*,
which has a very large circulation : he is an ex-director
in the Mexican Central road, and a capitalist largely
interested in railways and other enterprises. The other
gentleman has a large ship-building interest in Bath,
Maine ; he is president of the Eastern, and a director of the Mexican Central road. Their respective
partners at this game are both wealthy capitalists of
Boston, who are interested in various leading railroads.
One of these is senior member of a large grocery firm,
and the other, who from the color of his hair might be
taken for a much older person, is member of an old-
established mercantile shipping-house. The venerable
member of this party who sits at the farther end of the
parlor is a wealthy gentleman of Augusta, Maine ; he
is a director in the Eastern, and largely interested in
other roads. One other, sitting opposite, is also a
capitalist, and member of a Boston firm doing business
with Smyrna.

We have only time enough to pass hastily through
the Atchison car (No. 99), which we find almost de-
serted, the few occupants having retired to their rooms
to prepare for dinner, as we are now very near Topeka,
the capital of Kansas.

Our train arrived at Topeka at one o'clock P. M.,
and allowed us twenty minutes for dinner, which
awaited us at the station. This is a beautiful city of

about 25,000 inhabitants ; it is one of the most popu-
lous in the State, and for several years has been growing very rapidly. The general offices and shops of the
Santa Fé road are located here. Cars and engines and
complete trains are manufactured in this place. Members of a late editorial convention were carried on an
excursion by a train, every part of which was manufactured in these shops. Topeka is a city of wide
streets, beautiful public buildings, and fine residences.
The Kansas State capitol will be, when completed, one
of the finest in the Union. The Public Library Association has erected a beautiful structure for its use on
the capitol grounds, the money, $25,000, having been
donated by the Atchison, Topeka, and Santa Fé and the
Union Pacific railroads. Real estate is active and prices
reasonable ; indeed, Topeka is enjoying a " boom," and,
as becomes the capital of the most prosperous State in
the Union, is herself prosperous. *To-pe-ka* is an Indian
name, meaning " a good potato patch," — and it is a
good one.

We are already becoming accustomed to keep an eye
always upon our portable residences, lest they should
get away from us, for they stop and start again without
giving much warning ; so that an absent-minded person
might easily get left at some station, and find it impos-
sible to join us again, except upon our return trip — for
we are moving at a rapid rate, and making no unneces-
sary stops. But, of course, nothing of this sort is
likely to happen, for the party are in the habit of keep-
ing always together whenever we get out of the cars ;
and it is little enough to ask of each one to be sure
and get on when the train starts.

The train left Topeka at 1.30 P. M., and continued its course, stopping at Burlingame, Osage City, Emporia, and other important cities along the route, reaching Newton at 7 P. M. Here an opportunity was given for supper. Newton is an incorporated city, situated about two hundred and one miles from Kansas City, and is the county-seat of Harvey County. It is one of the most flourishing towns in the Arkansas Valley; it contains a population of nearly four thousand, and is rapidly growing; it is well provided with churches of various denominations; it has a graded public school, four banks, five good hotels, and two weekly newspapers. The southwest corner of Harvey County just touches the Arkansas River. This is one of the principal wheat counties of the State, averaging twenty-six bushels per acre. A splendid new station has just been erected here at a cost of $30,000.

Friday, May 2d. We have now passed out of the State of Kansas, which we entered yesterday morning, and have entered Colorado. We can now feast our eyes upon its vast plains, and form some conception of the immensity of the West. There is at times no limit to our view, excepting only the limit of our own vision. The landscape is a monotonous plain, relieved only by the low, blue line of distant mountains on the west, with the snowy crests of the Spanish peaks as the most prominent feature. Well has Joaquin Miller said : —

" Colorado, rare Colorado ! Yonder she rests ; her head of gold pillowed on the Rocky Mountains, her breast a shield of silver, her feet in the brown grass,

the boundless plains for a play-ground. She is set on
a hill before the world. The air is very clear, that you
may see her well. She is as naked as a new-born
babe; naked, but not ashamed."

Probably owing to the early season of the year, the
plains are now almost barren; little else than brush and
very short grass is now visible upon the earth's surface
for miles around; and when we see, now and again, large
herds of cattle and horses, we cannot help wondering
how these poor creatures manage to sustain life at this
season of the year.

We reached La Junta at 8.15 A. M., and here we were
invited to alight and partake of breakfast, which we
gladly did. No hesitation was ever felt by any one
about leaving the car, with our things all within easy
reach of any who might be disposed to appropriate
them; for our attentive and efficient porters were
always on hand, guarding the doors during our absence.
The dining-rooms were in a separate building, a little
way from the station, and connected with it by a plank
walk. La Junta is 571 miles from Kansas City, and
it is the junction of the Colorado and the New Mexico
lines of the Atchison road. It is a railroad town, with
a population of about 1,000.

We found it covered with snow, which was now
falling quite fast; and as we proceed, our course gradually ascending upon a very steeply graded road, we find
the ground completely covered with snow. There are
several small stations along the route, but few of them
have reached the importance of a post-office. Probably
the herders who ride over these plains do not devote

much time to opening the morning mail. Among other places we passed the city of Trinidad, which lies at the foot of Raton Mountains, 652 miles from Kansas City. This is the county-seat of Las Animas County, and was one of the most important between Santa Fé and the Missouri River in the days of the Old Santa Fé Trail. Trinidad is the first typical Mexican town met with on the southern route across the continent, and, with its mixture of wooden, brick, and adobe houses, is always an object of interest to travellers on a first journey to the land of the *burro.*

Morley, at the foot of Raton Pass, is the home of about sixty people, employed by the railroad company. Here another powerful engine is added, and the train begins to climb up the mountain on one of the best pieces of railroad-track in America. The grade is 185 feet to the mile. The ascent is attended with many charming views, not in the least marred by the name which attaches to the pass — "Devil's Cañon." The view afforded from the pass of the Spanish peaks, as they rise across the plains, nearly 100 miles to the north, affords an excellent illustration of the vast reach of vision which is possible in these mountain heights. The wagon-road, the same Old Santa Fé Trail, sticks to us, and runs close beside the track ; and it is not difficult to imagine the old-fashioned way of crossing the mountains, for down there on the right is "Uncle Dick Wootton's" great square house — an old stage station. This was "Uncle Dick's" Thermopylæ ; he kept the pass like a Spartan, and collected toll like the enterprising Yankee that he was. Five miles farther up the mountain, at an elevation of 7,688 feet, the train suddenly plunges into a tunnel nearly half a mile long, running under the crest of the Raton range. The light of Colorado quickly vanishes, and that which flashes upon us again in a few minutes is the warm brightness of sunny New Mexico,— for we have crossed the border while going through the tunnel. But stranger things than that have happened in tunnels.

The party dined at Raton, which lies at the foot of Raton Mountains, 675 miles from Kansas City. It has a beautiful site, and is so sheltered by the mountains that the cold is never severe, while its high altitude (6,688 feet) gives it a delightful summer temperature. The principal business here is coal-mining. It is estimated that there are 800,000 acres of coal-land in this (Colfax) County.

After dinner the train proceeded to Las Vegas, snow following us all the way, and we arrived at this place at about 6.30 P. M.   With a population of 9,000, Las Vegas is one of the principal cities of New Mexico ; it is situated 789 miles from Kansas City.   There are two towns, the old and the new ; the old town is built of adobe, and was one of the important stations of the Old Santa Fé Trail, as the new town is an important station of the new.   The Mexican population includes some of the wealthiest and most noted families in the Territory — families who have taken a leading part in all that has been done here for several generations.   An enterprising class of people from the States has settled in the new town, and the society of Las Vegas is such as may be found in any Eastern city.

A Catholic college, a female seminary, Las Vegas Academy, and good private and public schools, do credit to the city. Las Vegas is centrally located with respect to the finest and most extensive stock ranges in New Mexico, and the cattle and sheep interests are very important. The meaning of Las Vegas is *the meadows*, and a view of the landscape shows the place to have been appropriately named.

The famous Las Vegas Hot Springs are situated some six miles from the city, with which they are connected by a branch of the Atchison, running four trains each way daily between the Springs and the city. The climate is almost perfect; and situated at an altitude of 6,767 feet, the place of itself is an excellent resort for the sick. But the crowning glory is the water of the Springs, which is similar to that of the hot springs of Arkansas, and is possessed of great medicinal qualities.

Saturday, May 3d. A pleasant, sunny day is before us; the snow has disappeared, excepting only what may be seen here and there upon the mountain peaks, apparently not many miles away. The earth has assumed a reddish tint. All the little hills or ridges that we pass by seem to be composed of red sand or gravel, with little or no signs of vegetation. One of the places we stopped at this morning is called Socorro, and is one of the principal mining towns of the Territory, with a population of about 5,000. There is at this place, also, a new and old town. The old took its name from the story that "once upon a time," when a revolution was in progress, a party of Santa Fé Spanish fugitives received help here from their countrymen at El Paso. Hence the name, which means "succor."

We reached San Marcial at 8.15 A. M., and time was here given the excursionists for breakfast. The battle of Valverde, named after a little Mexican village across the Rio Grande, was fought here between the Confederate troops under General Sibley and the Union troops under General Canby, in 1862. San Marcial is 1,021 miles from Kansas City.

It was at this station that we were fortunate enough to fall in with the scout, author, and poet, Captain J. W. Crawford, familiarly known as Captain Jack. The Captain is a modest, but original and versatile poet, and is entitled to a wider reputation than he has yet attained. In a chat about the war of the rebellion, it appeared that Captain Jack was a member of Colonel Pope's regiment at the storming of Fort Hell, and upon arriving in Mexico, the Colonel (who was one of our party) received a pleasant letter from the scout, enclosing the following impromptu poetical tribute to his former comrade and commander : —

ACROSTIC.

Albert, here I wish you gladness,
    Always sunshine on your trail;
Pleasure banish care and sadness,
    Onward drive your flowing sail.
Peace be yours where'er you go,
E'en through strange old Mexico.

REMINISCENCE.

Comrade of the loyal legion,
We have met in hotter region,
Hell!—"Fort Hell," I mean—when fighting
For our flag, our country righting;—
You commanding, I obeying,
With my comrades ever staying,
Till that piece of rebel shell
Sent me limping from Fort Hell.

Here it was our gallant Potter
Fell amidst the fearful slaughter, —
Fell to rise again, God bless him!
See his loving ones caress him!
See his country's flag and ours
Floating high o'er freedom's towers —
Ours that day — a fearful tussle,
Won by Heaven and Yankee muscle.

Peace! good-will! a happy land,
Fraternity on every hand;
Charity, the soldier's boon,
Loyalty in perfect tune,
North and South and East and West —
All in unison are blessed.

J. W. CRAWFORD.

Formerly 48th Pa. V. V., late Chief of Scouts, U. S. Army.

The Rio Grande turns to the west side of the road
at San Marcial, and shortly after leaving the station,
we went over a fine bridge of the Atchison, Topeka,
and Santa Fé Railroad, which was still in process of
construction. Through the courtesy of Mr. Speare,
the managing director of the Atchison, a magnificent
view was now afforded from the rear window of (No.
99) the last car on the train. The country is some-

what irregular here, and the reddish tint of the hills or
ridges upon either side of the road, would seem to in-
dicate that the earth was impregnated with mineral
substances.

We reached Rincon at noon, and remained here a
little less than an hour. This place is the junction of
the El Paso branch of the Atchison road, which runs
down the Rio Grande, crossing into Texas when
within eighteen miles of El Paso. The excursionists
had a good opportunity at Rincon to explore the interior of some of the houses, shops, billiard-hall, and a
" hotel," all built of adobe, and ranged on one side of
the road opposite the station.

The train reached Las Cruces at 2.30 P. M. This is
the principal town between Rincon and El Paso ; it has
a population of 3,000. The town is very prettily situated at the foot of a very beautiful range of mountains,
one of which is named Organ Mountain, from its peculiar peaks of irregular heights, not unlike the pipes of
an organ. The valley of the Rio Grande here has the
appearance of being but a sandy, sage-brush barren ;
but we are informed that irrigation makes it the best of
soil for fruit-growing, and more particularly for
grapes.

Two hours' longer ride brings us now to El Paso,
Texas, the terminus of the Atchison, Topeka, and
Santa Fé Railroad—or, that is to say, the terminus of
this branch of that road. The population of El Paso
is about 3,500, and the city is growing very rapidly ; a
large retail and wholesale trade is done here ; there are
hotels, banks, and a street railway running across the

Rio Grande to the old town of Paso del Norte. The Atchison road connects here in its own depot with the Mexican Central Railroad.

There being ample time at our disposal, we left the cars and walked through the city, visiting the principal shops, many of them of great extent, and carrying lines of goods which would do credit to the largest concerns at home. Vast quantities of goods of American manufacture are received here and sent across the Rio Grande by mule trains at isolated points along the river. The contraband trade with Mexico is said to be enormous.

The tourists took passage in the street-cars, and went across the river to Paso del Norte, the " gateway of Mexico," which, though brought into prominence by its railway connections, is still the typical Mexican town. This we find a very different place from the bustling Yankee town on the American side — a quaint adobe town, embowered with verdure, threaded by irrigating ditches, filled with picturesque figures in colored *serapes*, in every way foreign to the eye. This is nominally the northern terminus of the Mexican Central Railroad, though the trains of that road now cross the Rio Grande, and connect with those of the Atchison, Topeka, and Santa Fé, in a union depot. At Paso del Norte are some of the most important buildings of the Mexican Central Railway. There is a large adobe station, with offices, built in the Mexican fashion, with an interior court; and there is also a large and well-furnished hospital for sick and disabled employees of the company. This building attracted much attention,

and was warmly commended by the party. The restaurant in the station gave us also evidence of its good
management. Here the Mexican customs officers sub-
mit the passengers to the usual annoyance of examin-
ing baggage; but, thanks to the influence of Mr.
Mackenzie, the superintendent of the road, we were
subjected to little or no inconvenience by this ordeal.
Having exchanged money at the station, we again
resumed our journey.

Sunday, May 4th. A night-run across the desert
lands between Paso del Norte and Chihuahua, brought
our train to the first considerable Mexican city. As
approached by the railroad, Chihuahua presents a picturesque appearance. Across the plain, in the clear
atmosphere of the Mexican morning, rose, above the
white and brown walls of the city, the twin towers of
its noble cathedral. It was Sunday morning, and the
entire party visited the cathedral to witness morning
mass. The shops were all open, and were driving a
flourishing business. In the plaza under the trees were
gathered fruit-venders, loafers, and idling Americans.
Women looking like figures from the Orient, were fill-
ing their brown water-jars from the fountain in the
centre of the plaza. All was life and animation.

The city of Chihuahua was founded in 1604, and is
the capital of the State of Chihuahua. It is 225 miles
from El Paso, and has an altitude of 4,600 feet. Nearly
all the houses are of adobe, — although the public buildings and some of the dwellings are of stone, — and are
built in the usual Mexican style, around a square or

court called a *plactita*. The city is supplied with
water from the river Churiscar, ten miles distant, by
means of an aqueduct built by the Spanish between the
years 1717 and 1720. It is built of stone and cement,
a large part being built upon great arches of masonry,
and is in a perfect state of preservation. The principal domestic articles of commerce are coffee, sugar,
rice, cocoa, spices, hats, shoes, cassimeres, blankets,
and *serapes*. The principal trade of the city is with
the mining towns to the west. The population is offi-
cially stated at 20,000. The streets are cleanly, and
good order and thorough police organization is preserved. It is said that the Cathedral of Chihuahua
was commenced in the year 1738 and finished in 1849,
at a cost of $750,000 — the proceeds of a special tax on
the products of the Santa Eulalia silver mine, which is
situated about fifty miles from the city. A clock,
illuminated at night, ornaments its dome, and its façade
is embellished with life-size statues of the Saviour and
the twelve apostles. In one of its towers is a bell
which was pierced by a cannon-ball at the time of Maximilian's invasion, in 1866. The Government mint was
formerly a church, and from its tower, where he had
been confined, the patriot Hidalgo was taken to execu-
tion, July 30, 1811, on the spot now marked by a simple
monument of white stone.

Leaving Chihuahua, Sunday afternoon, the train
sped southward through a country which was very
interesting. Barren stretches of plain, on which the
various plants of the cactus family assumed weird
and grotesque shapes, were succeeded by fertile val-

leys, where there was every evidence of great agricultural wealth and development. Stops were made at
Santa Rosalia, Lerdo, and other stations between Chihuahua and Zacatecas. At Lerdo, in the Laguna
County, the party were surprised at the richness of the
region. This is a prosperous town of 10,000 inhabitants, and the emporium of the cotton district, which
now yields 30,000 bales a year, all of which goes south
for consumption. The soil and climate are so favorable that the plants need renewal only every fourth or
fifth year, and with improved machinery and presses,
greater areas would be brought under culture, and the
ratio of production largely increased. It is safe to
predict that Lerdo will, in time, become the greater
shipping-point for the road than even Zacatecas, at
which it is expected that the freight receipts will soon
amount to $50,000 per month.

The clearness of the atmosphere on these tablelands
is wonderful. Mountains one hundred miles away seem
not more than twenty miles distant. The sky had a
loftier look than with us at home; the very breath of
life was in the air, which was invigorating in the extreme. Before reaching Zacatecas, the train passed
for miles on miles across a vast plain under cultivation.
For many square miles on either hand stretched this
enormous plain of rich-toned red earth. The artist
of the party declared that no brush could hope to put
on canvas the rich, deep tones of this wonderful red
plain, on which the sun shone down in full splendor.
The blending of the blue of the sky with the rich hue
of the great plain, was suggestive of new harmonies

of color. The view was closed in, in the remote distance, by purple mountains, whose tops were bathed in sunshine.

To reach the mountain city of Zacatecas from the plain, the road must needs climb a great many hundred feet; and the manner in which engineering skill has here conquered the topographical obstacles, elicited the warm praise of veteran tourists. Here may be found a series of "horseshoe curves," which are more wonderful even than the famous ones on the Pennsylvania Central. Our train climbed the mountain in the late hours of a glorious afternoon. At the summit there was a superb panorama disclosed from the platform of the observation-car. The view seemed like a peep into illimitable space. The setting sun gilded the tops of great mountains eighty miles away — mountains rolling up on the far-off horizon like the billows of ocean. No wonder that Mr. Church says that Mexico is superior to Italy in landscape effects. Members of the party who had spent years abroad could not find words adequate to express their wonder and admiration. "I would give $10,000 to the artist who could paint the view for me," exclaimed one of them.

From the mountain-top the train descended, in many long, sweeping curves, to the mountain valley, where the mining city of Zacatecas is nestled amid its huge, brown hills. It was the "Cinco de Mayo" (5th of May), the Mexican Fourth of July, and all Zacatecas was out in holiday attire. Several people had assembled to witness the arrival of the splendid train, and the Spanish vocabulary was liberally drawn upon to find terms fit to express the popular approval of the luxurious cars of the Americans. Many of the leading citizens and their wives and daughters were admitted to the train, and shown the wonders of the pretty buffets, with elegant inlaid panels and sleeping-berths. All night long crowds of wide-eyed peons clustered about the train. They were there at dusk, and morning light showed no diminution of their number.

In the evening the party took dinner at the Hotel Zacatecano — a large stone structure, two stories in height, and built in the prevailing style of the country, with an interior court. The building was formerly a convent, but had been confiscated by the Government. After dinner the party walked to the plaza "El Jardin," and were received at the palace by Don Juan Carnales, the acting Governor of the State of Zacatecas. The plaza was thronged with people — a wonderfully sober and polite crowd of men, women, and children. There was not a drunken man in the vast assembly; not a loud word was heard; and the visiting Americans were treated with marked courtesy. The plaza was like a dream of the Arabian Nights. Thousands of Chinese lanterns hung from the trees, or were festooned on cords. Several electric lights threw their greater wealth of illumination upon the throng; bands of music were discoursing a fine programme from a raised platform in the centre; and the picturesque costumes of the Mexican common people, full of color, accentuated with scarlet and crimson, helped make up a scene such as few of our American eyes had before seen. This was indeed a rare treat from the balcony of the palace, as we stood listening to the music for a few moments.

The great acqueduct of Zacatecas, the Pompeiian decoration of the exterior of many of the houses, and the convent-crowned mountain-top, were transferred to the sketch-book of the special artist of the party. The city is distinctively a mining town. From the huge. denuded hills have been dug hundreds of millions of silver dollars. This region must afford much business to the road. The freight-house at Zacatecas was crowded with goods and agricultural products, received on the Sunday before the national holiday, and outside stood a train of packed freight cars. In the freight house the party inspected tiers of cotton-bales,. the oval-shaped bales of native wool, and the packages of tobacco of Mexican growth. Zacatecas requires two car-loads of sugar per week, which come up from the City of Mexico — a sugar of native production and refining. Freight is increasing steadily at this point. No one can help seeing the business in plain sight. The local merchants are glad enough to have exchanged the slow *burro* for the lightning express, comparatively speaking, of the freight-trains. The great need of all the region is water; and with the perfection of great and extensive systems of irrigation, the country will blossom as the rose.

Tuesday, May 6th. Starting down the road in the morning, the train descended a sharp grade to another vast, red plain, also under cultivation. Several fortified *haciendas* were passed, and there was enough of interest to keep the eyes of the party strained for hours. It was a panorama of novelty and strange beauty. The train stopped at some of the stations along, and the tourists were afforded the opportunity to purchase delicious oranges, strawberries, pineapples, bananas, and other tropical fruits, from native venders who gathered at the station upon the approach of the train.

We rolled into Aguas Calientes at about noon. Mexico has a popular and growing summer resort at Aguas Calientes, 375 miles from the City of Mexico, in the mountains. The place is as high as the top of Mt. Washington, and the air cool and bracing. This is a lovely city of about 30,000 people, which lies on a plain, far across which may be discerned its graceful towers. The city of "hot waters," which its name implies, has been famous for centuries. Its thermal springs were places of resort for the subjects of the Montezumas — centuries before Boston was founded, or Columbus had crossed the ocean to open the way for bold Cortez. There are two first-class bathing-establishments near the railway station, to which the hot water is led through canals from the distant springs. By the time the baths are reached the water has become tepid, and pleasant for bathing. A single bath costs twenty cents, and a swimming-bath in pools filled by an overflowing stream costs twenty-five cents. Clean towels and soap are furnished by the polite attendants. Many of the excursionists tried the virtues of the famous waters, and were greatly refreshed thereby. The bathing-establishments are clean and attractive with their gardens and flowers.

A short stop was made here, and the entire party visited the city proper, a short distance from the station. The bells in the church-towers clanged out the hour of noon as the party arrived at the plaza in front of the City Hall; and immediately after, two trumpeters, clad in a fatigue uniform of white, emerged from the edifice, and added to the volume of sound which filled the vibrating air. The Plaza de Armas was thronged with idle people in white, and wearing broad-brimmed *sombreros*. The waters laved the basins of the fountains, the air was full of the rich perfume of the oleander-trees, while dark-eyed maidens in white muslins and mantillas glided along the walks, accompanied by their mammas or *duenas*. The Paseo, a lovely garden of large extent, was next visited. It is one of the most beautiful gardens in all Mexico. Shrill-voiced tropical birds sang in the branches of the lofty trees, while children chattered in musical Castilian below. The tourists were delighted with fair Aguas Calientes, the Saratoga of Mexico, and left regretfully.

Beyond Aguas Calientes the train sped on through a country dotted with *haciendas*, until the great bridge of Encarnacion was reached. This fine iron structure is over 1,000 feet in length, and 135 feet above the stream below. It was built in England, and is a substantial specimen of bridge-work. The train was stopped after crossing the bridge, and a portion of the party descended to the foot of the embankment, to get a clearer notion of the immensity of the structure.

The next stop of importance was at Lagos, a beau-

tiful town, surrounded by lakes, or *lagos*, from which
it derives its name. The land in the vicinity of the
place is under a high state of cultivation. The station
is of adobe, two stories in height—a creditable building.
The freight-house was visited, and the party had a
chance to witness the unloading of a train of ox-
wagons, which had brought in several hundred sacks
of salt to send off by rail. Diminutive peons would
take 300-pound sacks on their shoulders and tote them
to the cars, going up a sharp incline with firm step.

Another long stop was made at Leon, the second
city as to population in the country. Leon contains
120,000 souls, and in its immediate suburbs are 50,000
more. It is engaged in the manufacture of leather,
cotton and woollen goods, saddlery (for which the
place is famous), hats, cloth, boots, shoes, and cutlery,
and is surrounded by cultivated valleys. One cannot
fail to be impressed with the size of Leon, for it is
crowded with people, the streets are thronged with
peons, and there is every evidence of a great indus-
trial centre.

The party reached the centre of the city by means
of street-cars, riding through a long, Oriental-looking
street with houses of adobe built upon each side of the
road ; and they visited the fruit market, where a large
assortment of fruit could be seen, and with some varie-
ties of which our tourists became acquainted for the
first time. They also visited the theatre, which is one
of the finest in the country, only second to the Teatro
Nacional of the metropolis itself, and is, if anything,
more beautiful. The churches of Leon are large, and

very imposing in appearance.   There are a large number of extensive dry-goods stores;   also groceries, cigar, and wine-shops in abundance — the same general appearance everywhere.   One-story buildings predominate;   and dark-skinned people, men, women, and children, congregate about the low doorways.

Silao, with its domes and spires, was the next place of stoppage.   Here the train was side-tracked for the night.   Silao is a pretty city of 30,000 inhabitants.   It has large flouring-mills, and is the junction point of the branch line to Guanajuato, a city of 75,000 people, mainly devoted to mining interests, and which is the capital of the State of Guanajuato.

Wednesday, May 7th.   An early start was made this morning upon the branch road, to visit the richest mining city in Mexico.   Guanajuato is pronounced by old travellers to be unique.   Situated in a mountain gorge, its drab houses of adobe perched on the steep sides of the hills, it afforded to the artistic eye a great many attractions.   You cannot conceive of a more curious old town.   It has noble churches, a fine plaza, and a handsome market, though not so grand as the domed market of Leon; but in the Guanajuato market you see ancient Mexico.   The venders sit in Turkish fashion on the ground, with their wares spread out around them, and it is a place of animation.

The public school system of Mexico, fostered by the national Government, will soon raise, in a sensible manner, the level of popular intelligence.   Education for all is the policy of the Government.   In the per-

paratory schools, where pupils are too poor to remain
in school unassisted, the national Government comes
to their relief, and by pecuniary assistance to the par-
ents, enables the boy to get an education. The good
manners of the school-children of Mexico merit commendation. "Urbanity" is a school study as much
as arithmetic or spelling. There is a regular school-
book which treats of such topics as respect to one's
elders and superiors, the etiquette of the home and the
street. Thus carefully trained at an age when discipline is most required, the Mexican youth grows up
with good manners and courteous habits. It was indeed a pleasing sight, the exquisite manners of the
youngest children in the primary school of Guanajuato,
which we visited. Youngsters of four and five received
foreign visitors, clad in a garb which to them must
have appeared quite outlandish, without a murmur of
laughter, and with all the *aplomb* of cosmopolites.
Children in Mexico are kept in wholesome subjection
to their elders. Corporal punishment is the rule, but
parental discipline is tempered by that kindly familiar-
ity with the children of the household which is characteristic of Latin nations. Babies are wonderfully
numerous here. The quaint little brown faces of the
black-eyed infants of the lower classes peep at you
everywhere on the streets from out the folds of the
mother's rebozos. The Mexican baby of the lower
classes is out of doors a large part of its life. Some of
them are hungry-looking little pinched bodies, so
meagre as to excite your pity, yet are never heard cry-
ing. Perhaps this is an Aztec characteristic.

The tourist in Mexico should not omit to visit Guanajuato. Its massive, fortified reduction works, its
grand bits of masonry in the way of bridges, its aspect
of antiquity, and its Oriental character, will charm the
lover of the picturesque. OTHER
Returning now to Silao, a sumptuous " table d'hote"
dinner, such as only the French know how to prepare, was provided for the party at the station by the
little Frenchman who has charge of the restaurant.
The abundance and variety of the " menu " is beyond
ordinary ability to describe.

Coming down the road a stop was made at Celaya,
where the *dulce* (sweatmeats) venders swarmed about
the train, and the excursionists bought sweets, and ate
of mangoes and mamayas to their hearts' content.
Celaya has a population of 30,000, has extensive cotton and woollen mills and bleacheries. We were here
informed of the wrecking of the train which passed us
last night — a compliment which was undoubtedly in-
tended for us ; and we learned that the desperadoes who
attempted to wreck the train were being hunted. Three
of them have already been caught, and immediately
executed, and the Government will do all that is possible to quell the mob. Every man caught doing any
lawless act against this road will, upon proof of guilt,
be immediately shot. They are reported to be a band
of robbers. They derailed simply the engine, and shot
at the engineer, but succeeded in injuring only one
man, a Mexican, who carried a great deal of money
with him. A portion of the wreck was still upon one
side of the track when we passed the spot at 5.30 P. M.

A very brief stop was made at Queretero — a city containing a great many churches and 36,000 inhabitants, and where bigotry is intrenched still. It is a lovely city indeed, with a noble aqueduct, some of the arches of which are ninety feet in height. Three crosses mark the spot on the small hill north of the city where the Archduke Maximillian and Generals Miramon and Mejia were shot, June 19, 1867. Here is situated also the famous Hercules Cotton Mill, where 1,400 people are employed. Shortly after leaving Queretero, a fine bird's-eye view was afforded from the car windows of the mill buildings, boarding-houses, and the grounds surrounding them, as we passed on. The wealth of the rich Rubio family came out of this mill, which has its little standing army, and has resisted several revolutions. At night the train stopped at San Juan del Rio. This city has a population of 18,000, and is active and enterprising.

Thursday, May 8th. The train left San Juan del Rio at a very early hour in the morning. As the train climbs the low mountains to the south, we have a lovely view of the valley, of the distant mountains, and the great *haciendas* scattered along the plains at their feet. Upward through the broken and picturesque country, across the broad plain of Cazadero, and over the summit at Marquez, the train goes down in the Tula Valley, amid timber, and foliage, and evidences of approach to the tropics. Tula is full of interest for the student of antiquities, and has many relics of the Toltec civilization. It is a growing city of about 10,000 inhabitants.

As the train passed down into the famous valley of Mexico, the farms or plantations increased in number; the country grew more thickly populated; the purple mountains, which bound the valley of Mexico, shut in the horizon; and over all swelled the blue vault of the everlasting firmament. The valley of Mexico has been the theme of poet and historian; its beauties have never been exaggerated; it has been the theatre of the bravest deeds of men of arms, the scene of great acts, and of romantic exploits. Here nature matches the grandeur of history. The stage is ample for the grandest representations of human passion or courage.

The train sped around a curve, and entered the city of Mexico by the side of the " *Tajo de Nochistango*," the cut or trench, four miles in length, 30 to 160 feet deep, and from 200 to 300 feet wide, which was built in 1607, in order to save the city from inundation. There are no less than six lakes : Chalco and Xochimilco, the southernmost, whose levels are ten feet above that of Texcoco, the largest and nearest, but six feet below the pavement of the city at ordinary stages of the water; San Christobal, a small lake north of Texcoco, and Xaltocan, and Zumpango in the northern end of the valley, at an elevation of twenty-five feet above the city; and until this trench was made, which was originally made in the shape of a tunnel, the city was constantly threatened with inundation.

The towers of the great cathedral are now pointed out to us, and very soon we are in Mexico, a city which for grandeur of site has few rivals. The party was met at the station by Mr. Robinson, the general manager of the road, Mr. Lawrie of Boston, Mr. Camacho of Mexico, both directors of the road, and a delegation of the leading citizens. Mr. Camacho kindly placed his residence at the service of the visitors, and they were conveyed there in private carriages which were in waiting. The party spent the afternoon quietly resting, after their long, continuous ride.

The City of Mexico was a seat of art, science, and commerce, long before the Spanish Conquerors reached the shores of the New World. It lies in latitude 19° 26′ north of the equator, and at an elevation above the sea of 7,450 feet. The temperature ranges between 65 and 85°, varying little with the seasons; the mornings and nights are cool, while at midday it is invariably hot. The climate is strictly temperate, and the periodical alternations of rain and drought occur with regularity. The rainy season extends from June to November, and is the most delightful period of the year. Early in June all nature seems to look expectantly for the approaching shower, and dry, brown hills have been known to turn green in a single night; the beds of water-courses, which for months have remained perfectly dry, in a few days are transformed into channels of furious streams. The city is built on a part of the old bed of Lake Texcoco, and if not favorably located, science and art have done much to make it a beautiful city; and there seems to be a disposition among the authorities to make their nation's capital compare favorably with the capitals of other countries.

To a stranger, everything within the gates of this

ancient city seems curious and interesting: the manners, customs, dress, and the peculiar habits of the
people afford an interesting and entertaining study.
Since the advent of the railroad, however, the telegraph and the telephone — three of the most active
agents of modern civilization — the city has progressed
remarkably, many improvements being introduced,
such as gas-works, water-works, sewerage, street-
cars, and the electric light, by which some of the
principal streets and plazas are illuminated.

Speaking of the telephone, courtesy of intercourse
must be preserved even between invisible communi-
cants. The peremptory American method of calling
" Hello! hello! Give me 1235," etc. would never do
in the polished Castilian tongue, and the unseeming
vexatiousness and petulance which the telephone seems
to provoke in Saxon words, is never allowed to obtain
utterance here. The regular response from the central
office to a telephone call is " *Mande usted!*" which is
equivalent to " At your command!" Then prelimi-
naries are gone through something as follows : " Good-
morning, Señorita ; how do you do?" " Very well, I
thank you ; what service may I render you?" " Will
you kindly do me the favor of enabling me to speak
with Don So-and-So, No. 857?" " With much pleasure," etc., etc. ; and when the connection is made, the
usual polite introductories are gone through before
proceeding to the business in hand.

It is said that recent investigations show more
clearly that the City of Mexico at the time of the
Spanish conquest was situated on a small island fifteen

miles west of the present city, and connected with the
main-land by large causeways, composed of stones and
earth, through the lake. The circuit of the city meas-
ured nine miles. Monstrous dykes kept the water out,
canals were common, and business was largely conduc-
ted with the aid of boats. The markets were supplied
with the greatest variety of goods that could be found
in any market of the world at that period. When
Cortez entered Tenochtitlan he was amazed at the
mammoth temples, great markets, and the evidences
of civilization that were found on all sides. So much
for the early history of the city.

The principal street of Mexico, on or near which are
its largest hotels, its finest stores and restaurants, and
some of its richest private dwellings, is *Calle de San
Francisco.* In San Francisco Street are to be found
some of the most richly stocked stores in Mexico, where,
despite the almost prohibitory duties on foreign goods,
articles from every land on earth are accumulated.
Half way down the street is the principal hotel, where
some of the tourists found accommodations. As it
was once the palace of the Emperor Iturbide, after
whom it is named, it should have something stately
about it; and so it has. There is a high, sculptured
doorway of an Aztec touch in design, though not in
the details, and long, grotesque water-spouts project
into the street. Within is a large, arcaded court, from
which open *café* and billiard-room — the leading resort
of the golden youth of the town. The office is a dark
little box of a place, with two serious functionaries,
who seem to receive the visitor only with suspicion.

The gorgeous and affable hotel clerk of northern latitude is unknown here. In the rear are more courts, not arcaded, and around all of these the rooms are ranged in several stories.

We soon discover that Mexico is not a gay city. There are no crowds on the sidewalks, no eating of ices in public. By nine or ten o'clock the people seem to have retired, perhaps to be up betimes in the morning, for the work of the day. A military band plays three evenings in the week; but even these concerts, excepting on Sundays, are so sparsely attended that the men seem discoursing the music for their own amusement.

One never tires of the street-scenes in this city. They combine the commonplace, the pathetic, and the ludicrous; while in the eyes of strangers, the novel overshadows everything else. The peasant's gait is quick, and all his movements active. Short in stature and thick-set, he will, and often does, carry a burden of three hundred pounds, and go off with it at a jog-trot. There are no drays. Three men, and sometimes two, will carry a piano a dozen squares. In truth, the ordinary Mexican seems undaunted by tasks that would be undertaken by no other man. A crate of vegetables or fruit may be discerned jogging rapidly up some steep road, so huge that the bearer is quite invisible.

On the first evening, we went in company to the French Opera, where a very fair representation was given of William Tell, to a very small but select audience. Returning from the Opera, we brought up at

the first corner before a lantern on the ground, exactly
in the centre of the intersecting streets. "What is
that for?" was the natural inquiry. "That lantern?
Oh, that is a policeman's lantern. It shows that he
is in his place. Yes," looking around, "there he is,
behind that lamp-post. If he stirs so much as to
walk up to the middle of the block, he must take his
light with him; roundsmen are always on the watch,
and if lantern or man is gone there is trouble." Further observation showed that this explanation was cor-
rect. Every corner had its lantern exactly in the centre, and every lantern its policeman. Standing in the
middle of the roadway a long line of lights appeared,
stretching away to the four quarters of the compass.
The streets of Mexico cross each other exactly at right
angles, though each square has its individual name.
The main thoroughfare, from the plaza to the Ala-
meda, has as many names as blocks in the third of a
mile between the Iturbide Hotel and the plaza, and
doubtless as large a number off in the other direction.

The question is often asked "if the language of
Mexico is identical with the Castilian." We answer
in the affirmative. Of course there are some slight
differences in pronunciation, etc., but no more than
exists between the English and American languages.
For instance: in England they call a railroad-car a
"carriage," the engineer a "driver," the fireman a
"stoker," the brakeman a "guard," the switch a
"shunt," the track a "line," the baggage, "luggage;"
and yet the English and the Americans are supposed
to speak the same language.

Friday, May 9th. The visiting Directors of the Mexican Central Railroad and their friends spent this day, not according to any settled programme, but much as their fancy dictated. Until almost one o'clock most of the gentlemen remained in the parlor at Mr. Camacho's, and received distinguished visitors. Among those who called upon them are Gen. Porfirio Diaz, Thomas Braniff, Leandro Fernandez, Director of the Astronomical Observatory, and many other distinguished officials. In the afternoon a number of the gentleman took carriages, drove over various parts of the city, and visited Chapoltepec.

Towards the west, on the heights of Tacubaya and the plains of Tacuba, where the air is fresh and pure and the situation elevated, the city spreads, and grows more beautiful every day. Here reside many of the wealthy ; and here on the summit of this peak is Chapoltepec, surrounded by a grove of magnificent trees — hoary cedars and cypresses draped with Spanish moss. Chapoltepec is historic ground ; it was built and fortified by the first Montezuma, whose gardens stretched for miles around the base of the hill, was occupied by Cortez and by Maximilian, and was captured by the Americans, in 1847. Here are secret under-ground passages used by the old Aztecs, and later by the Spaniards ; and here is the military school, where three hundred young men are at present being fitted for a military career. Here, too, in the old part of the structure, workmen are engaged in preparing it as a summer palace for the-President.

The view from Chapoltepec is magnificent ; embrac-

ing the city and valley of Mexico, Popocatapetl and his
bride Iztaccihuatl, and the Paseo de la Reforma, a
boulevard two miles long from Chapoltepec to the city,
built by Maximilian, and bordered by a double row of
trees — Eucalyptus and ash.   This is the fashionable
drive of the city; and here the Mexican dandy is
a conspicuous figure, with his heavy spurs and
richly embroidered saddle, his trousers and *sombrero*
glistening with silver, and the cutlass and revolver
absolutely indispensable to complete the display.   At
the entrance of the Paseo is an equestrian statue of
Charles IV. of Spain — one of the largest and finest
bronze casts in the world.   Other statues are to be
placed at intervals along the boulevard; that of Columbus, which is already finished, is good work.

Messrs. Camacho and Fernandez accompanied the
party to the National Palace, and escorted them
through it.   The senate chamber, the various recep-
tion-rooms, the observatory, and different departments,
were all visited, and excited much interest.   A visit
was also paid to the Chamber of Deputies.   The Mexican President and the military commandant of this
district reside in the city palace.   Its most magnificent room is the Sala de Embajadores (Embassadors
Hall), which is 310 by 30 feet, with a throne at the end
for the President and his cabinet.   The walls are hung
with full-length portraits, by Mexican artists, of
Hidalgo, Morelos, and other heroes of the War of
Independence.   There is also a large painting of the
battle of Puebla, which took place May 5, 1862, and
portraits of Juarez, Diaz, and of our own Washington.

Messrs. Lawrie and Wilbur, Directors of the Mexican Central, who had been in the city some days in advance of the party, General-Manager Robinson and Superintendent Mackenzie, accompanied various members of the party on their trips about the city. Quite a number called upon United States Minister Morgan.

Saturday, May 10th. By daylight, with all its right colors upon it, and its normal stir of life going on, the famous capital is a very different place from what it is in the night. The visitor with an eye for the picturesque is charmed by a delicious feast of novelties, makes discoveries on every hand, and has the pleasure of testing the value of his own unaided conclusions. By little and little, misapprehensions are shaken off. After the first moment of disappointment we like it better, and in the end it takes a powerful hold.

A short walk from Hotel Iturbide brings us to the grand central plaza, in which events of such moment have been transacted. To actually sit down upon a bench in the midst of it, and gaze comfortably about — can it be possible? The imposing cathedral marks the spot where once stood the pyramid of the Aztec war god; and, as if to complete the triumph of the Cross, the foundations were laid with the broken images of the Aztec gods. These stones would be ankle-deep with all the blood of various sorts that has been spilled upon them. But it is hard to conjure up images of desperate conflicts, though here have been so many, in this bright sunshine, with the multitude of pretty, noble sights.

The cathedral, like most of the earlier architecture, is in the Renaissance style, somewhat inclined to the vagaries of rococo. It is saved from finicality, however, by its great size and massiveness, except in respect to the terminations of its towers, which are in the shape of immense bells. Adjoining, and forming a part of it, is a parish church, in a rich, dark red volcanic stone, ornamented with carvings. What a painting it would make on one of the perfect moonlight nights which bring out every line of the sculpture softly, and show the whole like a lovely vision. A magnificent view is afforded, from the cathedral towers, of the mountains and surrounding country. The cathedral was completed in 1667, at a cost of $1,762,000, and the towers were finished in 1791, at an additional cost of $194,000.

The interior decorations, paintings, furniture, and the services, are artistic in character. They were imported from Europe, and transported by wagons to distances varying from one hundred to six hundred miles, and at a great expense. The high altar, as well as the stalls of the choir, are beautifully carved, the former being gilded. Various notices invoking *paternosters* or *aves* for the repose of the souls of departed friends, or soliciting alms for certain purposes, are printed on paper of several colors, and posted on the main door of the church. The vestments worn by the priesthood while celebrating high mass are very costly, and consist of silken robes heavily embroidered with gold and silver thread.

Cemented into the wall on the west side of the Ca-

thedral is the Aztec calendar-stone, the most remarkable piece of sculpture yet disinterred. It consists of
a dark porphyry, and in its original dimensions, as
taken from the quarry, is computed to have weighed
nearly fifty tons. It was transported from the mountains beyond Lake Chalco, over a broken country in-
tersected by water-courses and canals. The fact that
so enormous a fragment of porphyry could be thus
safely carried for leagues, in the face of such obstacles, and without the aid of cattle,— for the Aztecs
had no animals of draught,— suggests to us no mean
ideas of their mechanical skill, and implies a degree of
cultivation little inferior to that demanded for the
geometrical and astronomical science displayed in the
inscription on this very stone.

Sculptured images were so numerous, that a new
cellar can hardly be dug, or foundation laid, without
turning up some of the mouldering relics of barbaric
art. But they are little heeded, and, if not wantonly
broken into pieces at once, are usually worked into the
rising wall or supports of the new edifice. Two celebrated bas-reliefs of the last Montezuma and his
father, cut in the solid rock, in the beautiful groves of
Chapoltepec, were deliberately destroyed, as late as
the last century, by order of the Government. The
monuments of the barbarian meet with as little respect
from civilized man, as those of the civilized man from
the barbarian.

One day, when first in Mexico, Cortez ascended to
the top of the *teocalli* and Montezuma, taking him
by the hand, pointed out to him the various parts of

the city. In like manner, let us ascend the cathedral
tower and look over the self-same valley, from nearly
the same height and point of view occupied by the
Spanish conqueror and the Aztec emperor. Elevated
at this height above the plaza, of nearly one hundred
and eighty feet, the din of the city reaches our ears —
the hum of myriad voices, the patter of thousands of
feet, and the rattle of coach-wheels over the pave-
ments. Directly beneath us is the great square, with
the smaller one, the *zocalo*, or pleasure garden, in its
centre. The latter is a green spot in this desert of
stone, its tall trees, shading marble walks, statues,
fountains, and flowers, beautifully disposed about a
central *kiosk* used as a music-stand. The flower market, occupying a small iron building of graceful architecture, is held here, and a small octangular structure
is the despatching office of the street railways, which,
radiating in every direction, reaches every desirable
suburb.

The tramcars in Mexico are all drawn by mules, and
when outside the city boundary the mules go at a fierce
gallop to their destination, the fare-collectors leaping
on board at a given point of the route. When ascending a hill no third mule is added, but, on the contrary, a horseman, waiting the arrival of the car at the
foot, urges the mules with whip and voice up the hill
with their burden. The conductors are smartly clad in
linen jackets and *sombreros* of gray felt, and are provided with a horn, which they sound at street-crossings,
or as a signal to the driver to pull up. There are first
and second class cars, the second class being used by
the Indians, and are often overcrowded.

Entering one of the first-class cars at the plaza, we went at a full gallop past adobe houses and *pulquerias*, the snow-capped giant Popocatapetl lifting his white head to the azure, on the right, and soon we reached Guadalupe, which is about three miles east of the city of Mexico. Through the avenue of trees the little church on the hill Tepeyac, erected where the Virgin is said to have appeared to the peasant Juan Diego, in 1531, and the cathedral at its foot, with its flat façade flanked by low towers, were both visible in the distance. The cars came to a standstill in front of the cathedral. This at one time was very rich in gold and silver ornaments, the offerings of the faithful; but many of these were confiscated and coined into money, by order of President Juarez, in 1860, and have since been replaced by inferior metal. There are, however, at this cathedral some rare statues — exquisite wood carvings representing apostles and saints, so life-like, that good authority pronounced them unexcelled by anything of the kind to be found in the cathedrals of Europe.

There is here, also, a sulphur spring, which is said to cure everything. The legend says that this spring of sulphur hydrogen gushed forth from a spot touched by one of the Virgin's feet. Faithful pilgrims coming here from a long distance, are often seen carrying back in bottles some of the water for future use.

The Jockey Club had invited members of the party to visit the School of Mines, the San Carlos Academy of Art, and the National Museum. They were accompanied by Mr. Thomas Moran, representing his step-

father, Mr. Sebastian Camacho, and he was untiring in
his efforts to promote the entertainment of his American friends. Among the other gentlemen who, on the
part of the Government or in their private capacity
accompanied the party to the public buildings referred
to, were Messrs. Velasco and Fernandez, of the Department of Public Works; Francisco de Garay, Francisco Soni, and Eugenio Barreiro of the City Council;
and Mariano Barcena, of the Meteorological Observatory.

In the court-yard of the Academy of Fine Arts of
San Carlos, our tourists were shown the carven sacri-
ficial stone — a huge block of jasper, with its upper surface somewhat convex. On this the prisoner was
stretched. Five priests secured his head and his
limbs; while the sixth, clad in a scarlet mantle,— em-
blematic of his bloody office,— dexterously opened the
breast of the wretched victim with a sharp razor of
itztli,— a volcanic substance, hard as flint,— and in-
serting his hand in the wound, tore out the palpitating
heart. The minister of death, first holding this up
toward the sun, an object of worship throughout Ana-
huac, cast it at the feet of the deity to whom the tem-
ple was devoted, while the multitudes below prostrated
themselves in humble adoration.

In the afternoon, some members of the party went
with Mr. Thomas Moran to the School for the Blind,
where a musical entertainment was given in compliment to them.

A banquet was given in the evening by the City
Council to the President and Directors of the Mexican

Central Railway, at which about one hundred and fifty guests were present. The entrance to the municipal palace and the historic hall of the City Council was profusely decorated, and thickly strewn for the occasion, with flowers and evergreens. The banquet-hall was also splendidly decorated with flowers and banners, and illuminated by electric lights. The fragrance of rose-leaves filled the air. The tables were lavishly adorned with the finest products of the floral world, and the banquet was luxurious in the extreme, including as it did all the rarities of the season, with wines of the finest vintage. The building, as well as the plaza in front, was lighted by electric lights, and presented a very fine effect. A fine orchestra delighted the ear with exquisite music, which was only interrupted, when necessary, to listen to the numerous toasts and speeches which were animated and eloquent.

The banquet was presided over by Senor Guillermo Valle, the President of the City Council. On his right sat ex-President Diaz, and on his left Mr. William Rotch, of Boston. Senor Valle made a speech congratulating the country on the completion of the road. He spoke substantially as follows : —

" The happy conclusion of the iron road between the capital of Mexico and the Northern frontier, has brought into intimate contact two neighboring Republics, the mutual interests of which would by this means acquire prodigious increase. This great work of progress and civilization demands from the Mexican people vivid expressions of their appreciation. For this reason the City Council voted to give this banquet to celebrate

the memorable event, and to offer a friendly testimony
to Mr. Nickerson, to whose enterprising spirit we owe
the completion of this great highway, and to his distinguished companions.   Finally, I hope for great felicity
for Mexico and for the United States, in the development of commerce and industry.''

Much regret was expressed at the absence of Mr.
Nickerson, who was prevented by illness from attending the banquet.   A speech prepared by him for the
occasion was read by Mr. William Rotch, and immediately after, a translation in Spanish of the same
speech was read by Señor Sebastian Camacho, the
Managing Director of the Mexican Central Road.

The speech was substantially as follows : —

Honorable City Council of the City of Mexico:

   " We are gathered here, by your invitation, to cele-
brate the conclusion of the Trunk Line of the Mexican
Central Railroad Company, which unites the city of
Mexico with the United States.

   " It is exactly one year to a day, since I visited this
city, and I then promised that, if possible, by the 5th
of May just passed, the two extremes of our Trunk
Line would be completed and united.   At that time
one end of the road was at Encarnacion, 323 miles
north of this city, and the other at Reforma, 358 miles
south of Paso del Norte — a total of 681 miles ; and it
gives me immense pleasure to say to you at this banquet, that the hopes which I then expressed have been
more than realized by the completion, on the 8th of
last March, of the 531 miles necessary to finish this
great international line.

"In the name of the Company, it gives me pleasure to acknowledge that the President of the Republic, the Secretary of Public Works, and all the distinguished gentlemen who constitute the Government with whom we have maintained constant relations, and who have invariably insisted that we should build a solid and secure road, have furnished us with all the facilities in their power to enable us to accomplish the great work. And now I feel happy at being able to congratulate this grand Republic, and this historical city, so noted for the many objects of interest that are treasured within its borders, for the happy termination of more than three years of assiduous labor which has resulted in the opening of a new field for enterprise and activity. How true it is that ' Peace hath her victories, no less renowned than war.'

" The victory has not been gained without struggle, for it has required the united efforts of the Directors of the Company and of the representatives of this Government, and also of the Managing Directors of the Company resident in Mexico, in order to conduct the grand enterprise to a successful issue.

" I should not forget, in this hour of triumph, the indefatigable labors of our deceased, but never-to-be forgotten friend, Ramon G. Guzman, who lent his incomparable aid to this Company, and whose death is to all of us the loss of a very dear friend and untiring co-worker.

"Our road is now open, and in condition to undertake the traffic of the country which is tributary to the line; and I have not the • least doubt that, within a short time, the Company will be able to adapt itself to the wants of the people. It is now in its infancy, and to obtain the best results for the country, as well as for the road, it will need the protection and support of this Government, and of the people; and I am convinced that it will be cheerfully granted in the future, as in the past.

"In behalf of my country and of this Company, I give you hearty thanks for the generous and cordial reception which you have given to your brothers from the North, on this, their visit to this country; and I entertain the hope that the iron bands which now embrace both countries will establish friendship, and make it more intimate; that it will enable the people to know each other better, and unite them with indissoluble ties like brothers, seeking the progress and development of the two Republics in knowledge, civilization, and prosperity."

A member of the party from Boston, in the name of his companions, was called upon, and proposed the following toast in Spanish: —

"General Porfirio Diaz, the illustrious protector of the Central Railroad, who, like Washington, is first in the hearts of his countrymen."

President Diaz was very much moved, and immediately arose to reply, saying: —

"It is indeed a great honor that has just been conferred upon me, by placing my own personalty by the side of that of Washington, a man, whose genius and whose virtues have merited and still merit the respect,

not only of all American citizens, but that of all
enlightened nations. I feel compelled, therefore, to
acknowledge my gratitude to the author of the toast,
for the good-will thereby manifested. Referring to the
Central Road, I did not hesitate, while discharging my
duties as President of the Republic, to grant the Company the concessions it has required ; for I was per-
suaded the grantee possessed the decisive elements necessary to carry out the enterprise to a successful issue.
I acted under this impression, expecting that time
would confirm my calculations. The work now accomplished has demonstrated that I was not mistaken, and
I think it is time now to cancel the promise, so to speak.
I have listened with emotion to the words expressed
in Mr. Nickerson's discourse concerning the labors of
the late Mr. Ramon G. Guzman ; and for my part I
desire to honor the memory of that indefatigable Mexican who toiled so assiduously to urge the construction
of the Central Road, and to endow his country with
important material improvements."

The remarks of General Diaz were most enthusiastically applauded. They were afterwards given in English by General Frisbie, who has been a resident of
Mexico for several years, and is familiar with the Spanish language.

Ex-Gov. Rice made a happy speech, comparing the
luxury of journeying in Pullman cars with the former
modes of travel, and proclaiming the consummation
of Humboldt's prediction that the table-lands of Mexico would become the great thoroughfare from the
North to the South.

Then arose the illustrious Mexican patriot, Monsignor Eulogio Gillow, who spoke in remarkably good English as follows:—

"*Gentlemen:* When I reflect on the great work that has been done, when I see our two great countries at last united by one of the most powerful ties that link human interests, I cannot but thank Providence for allowing, in the midst of so many difficulties, such a vast undertaking to be accomplished. Mexico, for her material and social welfare, required to be in closer communication with the rest of the world, and the North American Republic needed a more intimate intercourse with her Southern neighbor.

" The task being now completed, the glorious future lies before us. Let our mutual efforts remain united; let intelligence and manly energy continue to overrule our actions; so that the vast resources of the two countries may be profitable to both, and the surplus extend itself to the whole known world. The North, with her mechanical skill and inventions, will help Mexico wonderfully to develop her mineral and agricultural wealth, and combined production on a vast scale will, undoubtedly, bring about on this immense continent a commercial power in some future day of such magnitude, that it is not easy to foretell what will be its financial and political influence! Above all, gentlemen, the connection of the two countries will bring in contact and friendly relationship two nations that differ by their language, customs, and religion. May time unite them in one spirit—that of combined, progressive, and social interests; and in a higher point of moral view — that of a most perfect Christian charity."

One of the pleasant features of the banquet was the toast which Mr. Francisco Bermudez, Editor of the *Siglo XIX.*, proposed to the "Press of America." After paying a glowing tribute to the effective work which the newspapers of the United States had done to place Mexico properly before the world, he closed by citing, as a bright example of the press, the *Boston Herald*, which, with courage, intelligence, and ability, had ever stood by the best interests of Mexico. As Mr. Pulsifer, one of its proprietors, was present, he proposed a toast " to the *Boston Herald*, and Mr. R. M. Pulsifer, its publisher." This was most enthusiastically received. Mr. Pulsifer arose, and in a few words responded most pleasantly to the compliment paid his paper.

Eloquent and enthusiastic speeches were also made by Messrs. Prida, Camacho, Moran, and Friesbie in English, and by Messrs. Parra, Valle, and others in Spanish, until about midnight, when the guests left the municipal palace, and retired to their hotels. The lights were now extinguished, but the soft rays of the moon were much more in harmony with our feelings, and made a fitting close to the evening's entertainment.

Sunday, May 11th. Immediately after breakfast the party went, by invitation, to visit the house of the

late Mr. Guzman, who was a director in the Mexican
Central road. The house is very near the hotel. We
were cordially received by young Mr. Guzman, who
proceeded at once to show us the varied attractions of
the house. It is a large stone building, occupying a
space about one hundred and twenty feet square, built
in the usual Mexican style, with a *patio* in the centre.
In the lower part are located the stable, carriage-room,
and bathing conveniences. Over these were a succes-
sion of parlors, library, billiard, smoking, dining, and
sleeping rooms, all ranged around the open court in the
centre, and all connected with one another. A large
corridor overlooking the *patio*, and running all around
it, with tile floor, and ornamented with all kinds of
flowering plants, served the double purpose of indoor
garden and a means of access to all the rooms in the
house. The various rooms were very elegantly furnished, and most of them contained furniture imported
from Paris.

In the forenoon a number attended the Union Prot-
estant Church, where they listened to a sermon preached
by the Rev. Dr. F. A. Noble, of the Union Park Con-
gregational Church, Chicago. Others went to the Prot-
estant Episcopal Church, where the service was read in
Spanish by a Mexican clergyman. A visit was also
paid to the Cathedral.

Several of the party went down the canal in boats,
and inspected the floating gardens —*chinampas*, as they
were called by the Aztecs. These had their origin in
the detached masses of earth, which, loosening from
the shores, were still held together by the fibrous roots

with which they were penetrated. The primitive Aztecs, in their poverty of land, availed themselves of the hint thus afforded by nature. They constructed rafts of reeds, rushes, and other fibrous materials, which, tightly knit together, formed a sufficient basis for the sediment that they drew up from the bottom of the lake. Gradually islands were formed, two or three hundred feet in length and three or four feet in depth, with a rich, stimulated soil, on which the economical Indian raised his vegetables and flowers for the markets. Some of these *chinampas* were even firm enough to allow the growth of small trees, and to sustain a hut for the residence of the person who had charge of it; who, with a long pole resting on the bottom of the shallow basin, could change the position of his little territory at pleasure, which, with its rich freight of vegetable stores, was seen moving like some enchanted island over the water.

At two o'clock a special car, on the line leading to the Peralvillo Race-course, conveyed a large part of the American visitors to the grounds, where a special programme had been prepared for them by the Jockey Club. The day was a beautiful one, and the grounds presented a very attractive appearance. There was a large attendance, and the many brightly-dressed ladies who were present added to the effect of the scene.

Going to a race on Sunday was not just in accordance with the fixed principles of most of the gentlemen from New England, but they consoled themselves with the reflection that when in Mexico they were Mexicans; and therefore, as the races seemed to attract the better

class of Mexicans, they concluded to lay aside their
scruples and be present for the once. The races were
flat, excepting the steeple-chase. There were from
four to six entries in each race.

After the race, which excited much applause, came
what was a decided novelty to the visitors. About
five hundred yards of the race-track in front of the
grand stand was fenced in. Six or eight horsemen
with lassoes took their position inside this enclosure,
and near to where a gate opened into it from a small
yard which contained a number of bulls. These animals were let into the race-course one by one, and then
a pair of horsemen, with loud shouts, would run after
the frightened beasts, which would invariably rush
into another small yard at the farther end. The horsemen would clutch frantically for the tail of the bull,
and throw the creature down by a sudden twist. This
sport attracted attention for about an hour; then a
number of wild horses were let loose on the race-track,
and the men with the lassoes demonstrated how expertly
they could capture the animals. It was six o'clock
when the party returned to the *Café Anglais* for supper.

Notwithstanding the scruples above alluded to, there
was no lack of expressions of regret on the part of
others, that they did not improve perhaps their only
opportunity to witness a Mexican bull-fight; for there
was a bull-fight that same afternoon at Huizachal, a
small town a few miles only from Mexico, with which
it is connected by street-cars. Two gentlemen only
of the party were by fortunate circumstances enabled

to see this. So much has already been written upon this peculiar sport of the Spaniards, that we abstain from giving a full account of the fight. We cannot, however, refrain from saying that, admitting the numerous objections to the brutal tendencies exhibited throughout the different stages of the game, there was, nevertheless, much to admire in the hardihood and agility which was displayed by the men, from beginning to end, with so much ease and grace that the spectator forgets the peril, and is sensible only of the amusement. Bull-fights, or *funcion de toros*, usually take place on Sunday afternoons. They are forbidden by law within the city limits of Mexico.

Monday, May 12th. Another banquet was this day given at the Trivoli Garden of San Cosme, by Minister Pacheco, of the Department of Public Works (*fomento*), which was equally charming. The Garden, situated on the outskirts of the capital, is one of those earthly paradises which the favorable climate of Mexico permits man to establish. At this banquet were gathered many of the most illustrious men of the republic. President Nickerson sat by the side of General Diaz, opposite whom was General Pacheco, shot all to pieces in the war with the French. This old hero is minus an arm and a leg, and is maimed and crippled in a manner to have daunted any less intrepid spirit. He has been a warm friend of the new railway enterprise here, and has the confidence of the Americans to a marked extent.

Among other distinguished Mexicans were Gov.

Torres, of Sonora ; Señor Guillermo Valle, president of
the City Government; Senator Rubio ; Mr. James
Sullivan, of the Mexican National Railway ; Francisco
Bermudez, the Nestor of the Mexican Press, and a
publicist who has always been a strong friend of American enterprises here ; Editor Torres, of the famous
Monitor Republicano, the fearless critic of men in high
station. In all, some fifty of the leading men of the
capital were present. General Manager D. B. Robinson, of the Central Road, who has great reputation
here for ability and railway generalship, was also present. The speeches were full of friendly sentiment
toward the Central Road and the other American enterprises of like nature on Mexican soil.

The banqueting-hall was profusely decorated with
flowers ; and during the festivities music was furnished
by two of the most famous military bands of the
country, and national airs of Mexico and the United
States were sweetly blended. General Pacheco was
the first who arose to speak. He recited the difficulties under which Mexico has labored since her independence until the advent of General Diaz, to whom
is due the honor of initiating the new era in the
country. He praised the faith which had impelled the
Boston capitalists to invest their money here. He referred to the past as a guarantee for the future protection which the Government would afford the railway.
He concluded by proposing the health of President
Nickerson and his companions. He was warmly
applauded. General John B. Frisbie read the English
translation of General Pacheco's remarks, after which

President Nickerson arose. He was received with great applause, at the conclusion of which he said that he had prepared a few remarks for the occasion, but the state of his health prevented his presenting them. He had therefore entrusted the delivery of the same to Mr. William Rotch, who accordingly arose and read the following : —

" *To the Honorable General Carlos Pacheco, Minister of Public Works, and Gentlemen: —*

" We are assembled here to-day, upon your very kind invitation, to congratulate each other upon the happy completion of the main line of the Company, which now unites our two republics. It gives me great pleasure to recognize the honorable gentleman who presides at this banquet, as an officer of his Government, who, while always making it his first duty to be faithful and loyal to his country, has shown a readiness at all times to render to this Company all possible aid in the prosecution of its work.

" Allow me, esteemed sir, to thank you personally for all the aid and encouragement you have so kindly extended to this Company in the past. While congratulating ourselves upon our past work, let us look a little into the future of the country and the railway. In this connection, pardon me for alluding to the violent attacks which have been recently made upon the property by lawless men.

" While the Company is responsible for the safety of its passengers, it is powerless to protect itself from the attacks of such men, and we can only appeal to the laws of Mexico, without doubt that every effort will be made to guard and protect our road and its patrons. However, even this dark cloud, which has greatly disturbed our General Manager, has its silver lining.

"It is worthy of note, that for the past three years the correspondents of the press of Mexico, the United States, and Europe have written many articles upon the resources of this great country — your mines, agriculture, and manufactures of every kind; but to my mind they have overlooked the great value of your abundant labor. In looking over your country, we are astonished at the millions of hardy laboring-men in your midst — men of vigor and strength, inured to hardships from their birth, patient in their labor, who form one of the most efficient sources to which you must look for the development of your country. Of what value are mines and other resources without the hand of labor to develop and make them serviceable to the country and the world? In this vast number of laborers we find the silver lining to the cloud. To-day some of them think they see in the railway an enemy to their interests, but they will soon come to realize in it a friend and benefactor to themselves and their families.

 "Mexico now has the three elements of success : her own natural resources, the necessary labor for their full development, and the railway to transport her products to the markets of the world; and when these elements have found their proper relations, there remains no obstruction in the path of her progress and prosperity. Allow me to thank you for the

very kind and agreeable reception you have extended
to our people at this time, and assure you that we shall
take to our homes the most agreeable recollections of
this occasion."

Mr. Sebastian Camacho read the translation in Spanish of the above. Then arose Mr. Louis Mendez, who
made a few remarks. He traced the history of railroads in Mexico, and congratulated the Government
upon having so energetic and public-spirited a man
as General Pacheco in the Department of Public
Works.

Mr. Gonzalo A. Esteva made a very eloquent speech.
He welcomed the visiting party, and said that the hos-
pitality of Mexicans would always prompt them to
welcome such distinguished visitors ; yet when they
remembered the magnificent receptions given General
Diaz in the United States last year, it afforded all
Mexicans pleasure to, in part, reciprocate those court-
esies. He closed by proposing a toast to " the President of the United States," which was enthusiastically received.

Mr. F. R. Guernsey, of the *Boston Herald*, responded
to a toast, " The Press," using the " Castilian " as a
means of expressing himself. He said : " I am but
an humble servant of the Press, which, like the loco-
motive, is a powerful agent of civilization. We of
the United States of the North have enjoyed every
moment of our stay here, in the land whose earlier
history is embodied in the romantic pages of Prescott.
In conclusion, I beg to offer you the sentiment, *Viva*

the republic of Mexico, the hero Pacheco, and the
great statesman,— the Washington of his country, the
illustrious warrior,— General Porfirio Diaz."

Mr. Sebastian Camacho spoke eloquently. He said
that in celebrating the completion of the Trunk Line
which unites Mexico with the United States, he would
devote above all a few words to the memory of Mr.
Ramon G. Guzman, who contributed so largely to the
successful completion of the Mexican Central Railway.
After paying a glowing tribute to Mr. Guzman's memory, he did full justice to the American capitalists who
had invested their money in the great enterprise, and
to the Mexican Government, which has co-operated so
generously in the great work.

An informal meeting was this afternoon held at the
house of Mr. Camacho, and the party decided to start
on their return trip, Wednesday next, May 14th, at 3
P. M. The Directors of the Central Railway sent out
invitations to the members of the City Government
and other distinguished gentlemen of the city to come
and inspect the Pullman Buffet cars, which brought
the excursionists from Boston to the city of Mexico,
and which represent those which are attached to each
regular train between this city and Paso del Norte.

In the evening the visitors called on General and
Mrs. Diaz, and they were cordially received. Ex-
Gov. Rice made a few remarks in his happy style,
and, in behalf of President Nickerson, thanked General Diaz for his many services to the road, and
assured him of the high esteem in which he was held
by the American people. General Diaz, in eloquent

terms, acknowledged his pleasure, and gave assurances
that the Government would do everything in its power
to assist the road, and prevent recurrences of the
attacks which have been recently made on the road
by bandits.

Tuesday, May 13th. The tourists spent this day as
their fancy dictated. Some called upon United States
Minister Morgan. A number took dinner in the suburbs, by special invitation. Others went in quest of
feather-work and silver jewelry, for which Mexico has
been noted from time immemorial. Prescott, speaking
of the mechanical arts of the Aztecs at the time of the
conquest, says : "They cast, also, vessels of gold and
silver, carving them with their metallic chisels in a
very delicate manner. Some of the silver vases were
so large that a man could not encircle them with his
arms. They imitated very nicely the figures of animals, and, what was extraordinary, could mix the
metals in such a manner that the feathers of a bird, or
the scales of a fish, should be alternately of gold and
silver. The Spanish goldsmiths admitted their superi-
ority over themselves in these ingenious works."
"They could also enamel and make birds and animals,
with movable wings and limbs, in a most curious
fashion," says Herrera.

Referring to feather-work, Prescott says : "But the
art in which the Aztecs most delighted was their plumage, or feather-work. With this they would produce
all the effect of a beautiful mosaic. The gorgeous
plumage of the tropical birds, especially of the parrot

tribe, afforded every variety of color; and the fine down of the humming-bird, which revelled in swarms among the honey-suckle bowers of Mexico, supplied them with soft, aerial tints that gave an exquisite finish to the picture. The feathers, pasted on a fine cotton web, were wrought into dresses for the wealthy, hangings for apartments, and ornaments for the temples. No one of the American fabrics excited such admiration in Europe, whither numerous specimens were sent by the Conquerors."

Another extensive industry of Mexico is furnished by the *maguey* plant (*Agave Americana*). Prescott says in relation to this: "The miracle of nature was the great Mexican aloe, or *maguey*, whose clustering pyramids of flowers, towering above their dark coronals of leaves, were seen sprinkled over many a broad acre of the tableland. Its bruised leaves afforded a paste from which paper was manufactured; its juice was fermented into an intoxicating beverage, *pulque*, of which the natives to this day are excessively fond; its leaves further supplied an impenetrable thatch for the more humble dwellings; thread, of which coarse stuffs were made, and strong cords, were drawn from its tough and twisted fibres; pins and needles were made of the thorns at the extremity of the leaves; and the root, when properly cooked, was converted into a palatable and nutritious food. The *maguey*, in short, was meat, drink, clothing, and writing-materials for the Aztecs! Surely, never did nature enclose in so compact a form so many of the elements of human comfort and civilization!"

Pulque is the fermented sap, as we have seen, and is extracted from the heart of the plant. A single *maguey* plant, when it is fit for milking, will yield over a gallon of sap per day for about three months. It is of a milk-white appearance. It has a sourish taste, and just a suspicion of spirituous flavor. The taste for it is an acquired one. It is wholesome, and many people drink it for the sake of their health, but the great majority imbibe it solely for the sake of the *pulque*. The abundance of juice that may be extracted from a single plant is so much the more astonishing as the *maguey* plantations are in the most arid ground, and frequently on banks of rocks hardly covered with soil. Humboldt says the cultivation of the *maguey* has real advantage over the cultivation of maize, grain, and potatoes. The plant, with firm and vigorous leaves, is neither affected by drought nor by heat, nor by occasional severe frosts, which destroy the less hardy crops. One has to be very careful when going into a *maguey* field, on account of the scimitar-blade-shaped leaves of the plant, which stand in some portions of the ground as high as ten and fifteen feet, with bayonet-like thorns confronting one on all sides.

Wednesday, May 14th. The following announcement, which we find this morning in several of the newspapers of the city, and in various languages, will at least show that the interests of the "Arkwright Club" have not been neglected during the short time we have been permitted to remain in this metropolis : —
"An association of American manufacturers, repre-

senting the leading textile interests of the United States, were invited by the officers of the Mexican Central Railroad, on the occasion of the completion of that road to the Mexican capital, to send a representation of their products, with a view to further promoting commercial intercourse between the two republics. In accordance with this invitation, samples of such products are placed on exhibition for one month in the warehouse of Messrs. Watson, Phillips & Co., No. 10 Calle de Don Juan Manuel, where all information respecting them will be cheerfully given. Any citizens, and especially merchants and dealers, are cordially invited to inspect these goods, in the belief that careful examination will convince all parties that the progress made by American manufacturers has not been excelled by European producers of similar articles."

This morning, leave-taking calls were made on President Gonzalez and General Pacheco. After dinner the party returned to the station, and found their Buffet cars waiting to take them home. Fortunately it was not necessary to destroy the means for retreat by following the example of Cortez, who, for fear that on any occasion of disgust or disappointment the men might falter in purpose, get possession of the vessels and abandon the enterprise, came to the daring resolution to destroy the fleet without the knowledge of his army. This was not our experience. On the contrary, the same cars that carrird us to Mexico, with their respective porters, who now greeted us like old friends, were there ready to take us back to Boston.

The resources of the Buffet cars were very severely

taxed for an hour before leaving the station, during
the informal reception which was tendered to our Mex-
can friends; but they were fully able to supply every
demand. At 3.30 P. M. we bade farewell to our
friends, and quietly rolled out of the station, bound
towards home. Our party is now increased by the
addition of Mr. and Mrs. President Nickerson, Mr.
Lawrie, Mr. Wilbur — both Directors in the Mexican
Central Railroad, — General Manager Robinson, Mr.
Thomas Moran, and Mr. Charles C. Blodgett.

Mexican crowds afford a curiously interesting study
for American visitors. The first thing that strikes one
is the absence of jostling, and the regard for the rights
of every one by every one. There is no loud or bois-
terous talk. Women may walk the most densely
crowded streets of the city with greater certainty of
immunity from insult, than in Boston or New York.
A deferential courtesy is the rule here. The com-
monest peons lift their hats to one another. Whatever
infirmities of temper or character the Mexican people
may possess, their street-manners are a model for us.

It is commonly asserted that the lower classes of the
Mexican people are not honest; that they will commit
theft at every opportunity. But the Americans long
resident here say that they find their servants faithful
to their trust. That the peon of the street is likely to
walk off with any stray article which may come in his
way, is true; but we must bear in mind that these poor
people labor under extraordinary temptations. They
are bitterly poor, and the smallest trifle looks very
large to men and women who subsist on ten cents a

day. The peon class must, nevertheless, be the bulwark
of Mexico. Industrious, temperate, working uncom-
plainingly at the most menial and hardest task, cheer-
ful, kindly to one another, the despised peon will yet
become the foundation of the future great nation.

Café life is a feature of the metropolis. The restaurants are decorated with mirrors in the French style,
and the food is both good and cheap. Good table
board is provided at several places at one dollar per
day. The bread commonly eaten is a little, elongated,
hard-crusted biscuit, apt to be a trifle sour within.
The water is bad ; the wine universally good, and often
superior. The meats are fairly good, and a small but
well-cooked beefsteak can be obtained for twenty-five
cents. The coffee, which is of native growth, is palatable. As regards the chocolate which is largely drunk
here, it would be hard to speak in sufficient terms of
commendation. With a bun, called "*pan dulce*," and
a cup of chocolate, the Mexican gentleman makes a
comfortable "*desayuno*," or first meal at his *café*. A
cup of chocolate, a *pan dulce*, and an excellent omelet,
costs just thirty-seven and one-half cents. Rents are
high in Mexico, but food is cheap. The abundance of
fruit is a feature of the Mexican table. Every one eats
a great quantity of fruit — oranges, mangoes, melons,
apricots, peaches, bananas, etc. Sweets of every possible flavor are universally eaten. Many of the *dulces*
made by the peons are sold under their straw-canopied
stands ; and they are not only sold very cheap, but are
also delicious.

The city of Mexico cannot be hastily "done," and

therefore this cursory sketch can only give a faint idea.
It abounds in surprises, and cultivated and travelled
Americans long resident here are continually finding
new places of interest for exploration and investiga-
tion. Mexico is very old, and it has not yet become
modernized. Although this capital has a distinctly
metropolitan air, it still has a flavor of antiquity about
it, and is as full of romance as some of the most noted
places of Europe. Manners and customs, language,
architecture, street-scenes — all are full of novelty.
The visitor feels as if he were a participant in some
operatic scene, so utterly foreign is everything : streets
thronged with picturesque figures in brightly colored
serapes; water-carriers, with their jars lashed to their
heads ; soldiers ; bands of music ; houses built as strong
as castles ; mountains looming up at the end of every
street ; and over all, dominating all, the twin volcanoes,
crowned with never-melting snow, gilded by the
morning sun, and tinted with rosy pink at evening
— this is the city of Mexico.

There is probably no man in Mexico who grasps
more intelligently the great problems which confront
his nation, than does General Diaz. Cherishing a profound desire to receive the applause of foreign nations
by aiding the rise of his country in the scale of civilization, honorably ambitious, proud of his nationality,
firm as a ruler, and just in the application of the law,
he may be truly said to be the " hope of Mexico." He
has, by marriage into one of the old governing families
of the country, secured the alliance of a powerful class ;
but at the same time he has retained the sympathy of

the common people from whom he sprang. He is the most popular man in Mexico. He is not faultless, but he lives up to the light of his knowledge, and has the iron hand under the velvet glove which is needed to manage the helm of the Mexican ship of State.

General Diaz discerns the vast social revolution which has been started in his country. He sees clearly what the new railways mean; he knows that they mean the intercourse of Mexicans with men of Northern civilizations, comparisons of institutions, the introduction of new methods in the arts, the quickening of the aspirations of the lower classes for education, and a pressure of modern ideas on the higher classes too powerful to be resisted. The adjustment of the masses of the Mexican people to the new condition of things will naturally and inevitably be attended with some friction. We must be patient with Mexico, but the result may be looked for with confidence. A certain section of the American press is inclined to treat our sister nation with undeserved contempt. Her local disturbances are grossly exaggerated; her public men are given no credit for a particle of disinterestedness; and epithets are employed in a manner which must irritate a proud-spirited people.

The safety of the new *régime* in Mexico lies in the elevation of the lower classes. The people desire peace to continue. They have already had a taste of the delights of tranquility, and they want no more wars. With four more years of peace under the administration of General Diaz, we may hope never again to hear of revolution in Mexico.

The Mexican people have grasped the abstract idea of liberty, but they have not yet secured the practical realization of popular freedom. That realization will come. Education and the railways will develop a middle class ; the poverty of the masses will be ameliorated ; popular elections will be something more than a form ; a true system of local representation in congress will be obtained ; the army will cease to be the chief power in the State ; and Mexico will become in reality a republic. The patience of friendly and sympathizing nations will, before this result is attained, be often tried, perhaps ; but no true American can help entertaining a profound sympathy for a sister nation working out for herself the great problem of self-government.

These were some of the reflections which forced themselves upon the mind of each one of the party as he resumed the inactive state, once more, as a passenger in one or the other of the Buffet cars, while leaving the old city of Mexico for home.

Thursday, May 15th. The train stopped at San Juan del Rio for the night, and started again early this morning, reaching Queretaro at about 8.30 A. M. An opportunity was now given the party to visit the famous Hercules Mills. Don Cayetano Rubio, the present manager of this vast establishment, himself met us at the station, which was very near the mill-grounds, and accompanied the vistors through the factory.

This factory was begun in 1840 by Señor Rubio, the

father of the present incumbent. The cost of building it, together with the grounds, was $4,000,000. It is a sort of citadel. Enclosed by a high wall provided with port-holes, occupying several acres, and giving employment to 1,400 operatives, it forms a manufacturing town of itself. The Rubio family live here, and their apartments adjoin a beautiful garden laid out with artificial ponds and ornamented with statues. The buildings are of stone, and the machinery has been imported principally from England. Both steam and water power are used, and it has one of the largest overshot wheels in the world, being fifty feet in diameter. They keep a small "army" of forty soldiers, who are provided with muskets and howitzers. Thus far the owners have defended their property successfully against the insurgents during several revolutions.

A short ride in the street-cars brought us to the city of Queretaro, about two miles farther, and where our train had gone to wait for us. An amusing incident is related by a gentleman who recently returned from Queretaro. Calling upon a resident, who owned a most pronouncedly Scotch name, he addressed him in English. The reply came in Spanish: "For three generations my ancestors have lived here, and I cannot speak a word of English. I will call my sons: they speak English well, for I sent them to the mother country to learn it."

The journey home from this point was made as quickly as possible, there being some in our party who were a little indisposed, and therefore were anxious to reach their homes. The places we stopped at were principally the same that were visited on our way to Mexico ; so there is little if anything new or interesting to relate about them. General-Manager Robinson did his best to get the party off the Mexican Central Road as quickly as possible, making the last 720 miles in twenty-four hours. We reached Paso del Norte on the morning of Saturday, May 17th. Four gentlemen of the party, Messrs. Alden, Pierce, Jones, and Sewall, left us at this point, and went to California for a little trip before returning home.

Now bidding farewell to General-Manager Robinson, who goes back to Mexico, we cross the Rio Grande to El Paso, where our baggage has to go through the usual formalities with officials of "Uncle Sam's" dominions ; and, as some of the party remarked "We are once more in God's country." Whether this be true or no, there is one thing sure, we are no longer foreigners.

A few remarks in relation to the Mexican Central Road will not be inappropriate ere we close this journal. The survey made of the road was careful and impartial. A number of the party were capitalists, with no interest in the securities of the Company, and they all concur in one opinion : that the Central's enormous length of road is destined in the near future to be a first-class piece of railway property. Every one expressed admiration at the solidity of the road's construction, its smoothness and skilful engineering achievements, whereby many great difficulties have been overcome. The bridges, which are of iron, are of the latest approved pattern. What is of more immediate interest is, that the natives are using the trains freely. We continually noted the fulness of the trains that we passed along the entire length of the road. The wealthy Mexicans are taking eagerly to the luxurious Pullmans, and not infrequently hire a whole car for themselves and families. The railway has given a powerful impulse to visiting between cities formerly many days' distance from one another. There is no reason to doubt the large use of the passenger equipment of the Company.

In regard to derailments, most of the reports telegraphed to the United States in relation to them have been wildly sensational and exaggerated. However, they do not seem to interfere with the increase of tourists from the United States. An agent of the Rock Island Road says that he has arranged for an excursion party of one hundred rich Mexicans and their families to come to this country over the Central. They will visit Niagara Falls, New York, Philadelphia, and Washington, returning over the Central; and similar excursions will undoubtedly follow thereafter.

The higher class of the Central's officials appear to be endeavoring to forward the Company's interests. The financial crisis in Mexico necessarily interferes with the movement of business, but in the face of all this the freight traffic is increasing. The road-carriers, who used to do the work of transportation, and have been displaced by the railroad, are now largely engaged in developing the freight business between the railroad and points from twenty to one hundred miles

on either side. The owners of estates are increasing
their acreage. They are said to be selling off their
mules, and shipping their products by rail. On the
expiration of existing contracts with mule-freighters
to the city of Mexico, other owners of large estates
will transfer their freights to the Central. With the
completion of the side lines to Tampico and Guadala-
jara, there is no danger in hazarding the prediction
that the Central's business will be largely increased.
Cattle shipments are steadily increasing on the Central,
it being found that cattle lose less in weight when
going to the city of Mexico by rail. There is, therefore, no doubt of the steady growth of the herding
interests in the Mexican tablelands, and a correspond-
ing augmentation of freight receipts of the Central.
The leading articles of freight on the road, at present,
are cattle, coal, cotton, tobacco, dry goods, sugar,
and mining supplies. Arrangements are now making
for the bringing of coal from America to the large
interior cities of Mexico, which are beginning to realize the advantages of using coal in place of the costly
wood or charcoal which they have hitherto used as a
household cooking-fuel.

The Mexican Central Railway Company has a road
which is creditable in construction. By a series of
remarkable engineering gymnastics it climbs the mountains of Zacatecas, and the notched rim of the Valley
of Mexico. The contortions of the railway line in
reaching Zacatecas add very much to the interest of
the tourist. " Horse-shoes," as bends of that form are
usually called, are not only common, but in some in-

stances doubled; but with these exceptions the Mexican Central Road seems, strangely enough in so mountainous a country, to traverse a vast plateau. The business of the road is steadily increasing, and the rich land-owners through whose extensive estates the railroad runs are among the staunchest friends of the enterprise.

There is now but little more to add to this already too lengthy diary. Leaving El Paso on the forenoon of Saturday, May 17th, and making the usual stops, we reached Kansas City, the terminus of the Atchison Road, on the afternoon of Monday, the 19th. The train was detained only a little, on account of the Rio Grande, which was very much more fierce now than it was when we went over it before; the beds of water-courses, which before were perfectly dry, were now channels of furious streams, causing some wash-outs, and it required a careful running of the train. The little time that we had at Kansas City was improved by nearly every one of the party in riding about the various places of interest in this enterprising city.

Tuesday, May 20th. Those who were fortunate enough to awake early, found plenty upon which to feast their eyes, for a few moments at least, while crossing the Mississippi River, at about 5.30 A. M. We arrived at Chicago in the afternoon, and the party were given an opportunity to view this grand city. A large number of the tourists went to visit Pullman, the unique little town which has been built up by the Pullman Palace Car Company.

Several of the party left us at Chicago, and the remainder reached their homes on the morning of Thursday, May 22d, having accomplished the journey to the city of Mexico and back in less than twenty-four days, including six days spent in the old historic city of Mexico, the mother of Western civilization.

In conclusion: Mexico is now accessible as she has never been before, and abandoning all ancient antagonisms of race and customs, she invites every comer from the United States, the land of her ideals, asking for no passports and making no inquiries. The country has heretofore presented many obstacles to even the adventurous American traveller; it has been fenced in by rocky barriers, mountain chains, and immense distances more impassable than any sea, by lack of information concerning it, and by all differences of race, language, and custom. It was, moreover, the land of countless revolutions and political uncertainties, where the bandit or highway robber held triumphant sway. This has all been so far changed since the completion of the Mexican Central Railroad, that the requisites now of a most delightful journey are merely a through ticket and return, and a berth in a Buffet car.

The country is delightful, and undoubtedly repays a visit. Of tropical latitude, but of immense elevation, the climate remains the same through winter and summer. Tropical fruits are the usual products of every month in the year. The inner man may be surprised here with strange beverages, and the palate be accustomed to dishes hitherto unknown.

Every Mexican, of every grade and class, will be found to be a courteous man. Ask a Mexican gentleman a question on the street, and he will shake hands with you on parting. People whom you never saw before, and will in all probability never see again, will willingly show you every attention, simply because you are a stranger. There are thiêves, and some very ingenious and inveterate ones ; but, is there a country on the globe that is free from them?

Americans are, in certain things, the most inconsiderately impatient of all people. When we go to Mexico, which is one of the slowest countries on earth we shall have a much better time if we do not try to reform the country. We should avoid the impatient gesture, the disgusted look, and the pushing demeanor which accomplishes nothing, and bear in mind that we are in the land of *mañana* and *luego*. Since we must wait, more or less, we may as well be patient and philosophical about it.